JOHNNY DELGADO

KEVIN BROOKS

This one's for you,

First published in 2006 in Great Britain by
Barrington Stoke Ltd
18 Walker Street, Edinburgh, EH3 7LP

www.barringtonstoke.co.uk

This edition first published in 2016

A CIP catalogue record for this book is available
from the British Library upon request

ISBN: 978-1-78112-550-2

Printed in China by Leo

PART 1: PRIVATE DETECTIVE

PART 2: LIKE FATHER, LIKE SON

PART 1
PRIVATE DETECTIVE

CHAPTER 1
THE MOST BEAUTIFUL GIRLS IN THE WORLD

It all began with a bit of a problem. It was Friday evening, about six o'clock, and I was sitting by the desk in my bedroom. My bedroom's small, and the flat's small too. It's on the 17th floor of a South London tower block. Rain was drizzling on the window, and the air inside felt hot and steamy.

But that wasn't the problem.

The problem was this. The Most Beautiful Girl in the World was sitting on my bed, and the Second Most Beautiful Girl in the World was sitting next to her. And they were both wearing very tight clothes.

That was the problem.

Their names were Carly (Most Beautiful) and Bex (Second Most Beautiful). They'd been sitting on my bed for the last 20 minutes or so. They were telling me about a kid called Lee Kirk. I *think* that's what they'd been telling me about. It was hard to concentrate with the two Most Beautiful Girls in the World sitting on my bed.

"So," Carly said to me, "what do you think?"

"Uh?" I said back.

"What do you *think*?" she said. "Do you want the job or not?"

"What job?"

She shook her head. "We just *told* you. What's the *matter* with you? We told you all about it five *minutes* ago."

That's how she talked – sneering all the time, as if everything she talked about was stupid. And when she sneered, her lip curled up at the corner. Somehow that made her seem even more beautiful.

"What are you looking at?" she sneered at me.

"Nothing," I said. "I'm sorry. I was just –"

"What?" said Bex. "You was just *what*?"

I didn't know what to say to that, so I just sat there and stared back at my desk. The thing is, I knew they weren't *really* the Most Beautiful Girls in the World, but girls didn't come into my bedroom that often ... if you know what I mean. It made me feel weird and confused.

Carly was about 17, I'd guess. She was tall and slim, with glossy brown hair and stunning blue eyes. She had that look about her ... you know, the kind of look that makes you feel wobbly and stupid. Bex was younger, about the same age as me – around 15. She was short and blonde, with big full lips and curves everywhere. They both had lots of make-up on, and they were both chewing gum, loudly. And, like I said, they were both sitting on my bed in *very* tight T-shirts and jeans.

"Listen," said Carly with a sigh, "all I want you to do is find out if Lee's seeing this girl."

"What girl?" I said.

"The girl I just *told* you about."

"Oh, yeah ... right. And Lee's your boyfriend?"

"Yeah," Carly said, "he's my *boyfriend*."

"Lee Kirk."

"Yeah, Lee Kirk. I want you to follow him tomorrow night and see where he goes." Carly took a photo out of her pocket and passed it to me. "That's him," she said, "in the photo. And I've put his address on the back. He lives in the West Tower. 14th floor."

The photo was of a hard-looking bloke with small dark eyes and scratty blond hair. I'd seen him around the estate. I knew who he was.

"I'll be with him till seven," Carly told me, "and then he's supposed to be going out with his mates."

"But you think he's seeing this girl?"

"Yeah – she's an ugly little bitch called Tanya Nicols. She lives in the West Tower, too. On the second floor. I want you to wait for Lee on the 14th, then follow him down and see where he goes. If he goes into her flat, wait around and see how long he stays. If they go out, follow them." She sniffed, snapped her chewing-gum, then wiped her nose with the back of her hand. She gave me a look. "Do you think you can handle that?"

"Yeah," I said, "I think so."

"Good." She put her hand into her jeans pocket again. This time she pulled out a handful of cash. "How much d'you charge?"

Another problem. For some time now, I'd been putting the word out around the estate that people could hire me as a private detective. Yeah, I know it sounds weird. I'll tell you more about why and all that later on. Right now I want to tell you about this next problem. The problem was this. So far, no one *had* hired me. So I hadn't really thought about how much money to charge people for what I did. But I didn't want Carly and Bex to know that, did I? I had to think pretty quickly. How much should I charge?

"Well," I said, "it depends ..."

"On what?" said Carly.

"I don't know. How long do you think it'll take?"

Carly shook her head and looked over at Bex. They both smirked at each other, like they knew I was just making it up.

"What's the *most* it's going to cost?" said Carly.

"I don't know ..."

"Say it takes you five hours."

"Five hours?" I asked.

"Yeah – seven till twelve. You follow Lee for five hours. How much d'you think that'll cost?"

I had to stop hesitating. So I just picked a figure out of thin air. "Fifty quid?" I said. Carly nodded. She counted out some notes and passed them to Bex.

Bex got up and came over to me. I couldn't help watching the way that she walked – wiggling hips, wiggling curves, wiggling everything. She wiggled right up to me and dropped the money on the desk beside me. Then she put her hands on her hips and just stood there staring at me. Big full lips, lots of curves.

"Where's the bathroom?" she said, and she looked at Carly.

"Uh?"

"The *bathroom*. Where is it?"

My face went red. "Uh ... just down the hall," I told her. "On the left."

She grinned at me, then turned round and wiggled her way across the room and out the door.

I looked over at Carly.

She was grinning at me. I smiled at her. Her grin vanished.

"What you looking at?" she said.

I shook my head. "Nothing."

CHAPTER 2
STUPID

After Carly and Bex had left, I stayed in my bedroom for a while and thought about what I'd just done. *What had I done?* Well, I'd got myself a job, my first *paying* job. I'd just earned myself £50 for a few hours' work on a Saturday night. *That's* what I'd done. But did I feel good? No, I didn't. I didn't feel good at all. Because, basically, what I'd just done was plain stupid.

I hadn't thought things through.

I'd been too busy thinking about other things – tight clothes, curves, trying to look cool.

And, worst of all, I'd broken my rules.

You see, when I first decided to become a private detective, I set myself three simple rules.

Rule 1. Never get involved with relationship problems.

Rule 2. Never get involved with the local gangs.

Rule 3. Never get involved with the police.

They weren't difficult rules, and they made good sense. Relationship problems are tricky. The gangs are dangerous. And the police ... well, if you get involved with the police around here, you're just asking for trouble.

So, if I stuck to the rules, I had no worries. No danger, no trouble.

Nice and simple.

Right? Yeah, right. So what do I do when I get my very first job? What do I do? I break at least two of the rules, that's what I do.

Stupid stupid stupid.

I'd just said I'd follow someone who was most likely cheating on his girlfriend.

Stupid.

This someone was a kid called Lee Kirk. And Lee Kirk was a big name in one of the local gangs.

Stupid.

And if he spotted me following him, there was a good chance he'd beat the crap out of me. Then the police would start asking questions.

Stupid.

Yeah, so I felt pretty stupid. But that was nothing to how bad I was going to feel later on, when I found out what was *really* happening.

I was still in my bedroom when Mum came home. It was about seven o'clock. I wasn't doing anything special – just standing at the window, looking out at the rain. Right across from our tower block I could see the other two tower blocks on the estate – the East Tower and the West Tower. Grey concrete, grey glass, grey everything. I scanned the rows of windows. Was there anything happening in the other two tower blocks? All I could see were the dull reflections of the clouded sky in the glass.

I looked down.

Seventeen floors below, the estate was cold and empty in the rain. There wasn't much to see. A couple of cars parked at the back of the lock-up garages. Some kids from the East Tower slouching along Newton Lane. A skinny Alsatian dog skulking around the benches.

My door opened, and I turned round.

"Hey, you," said Mum. "How's it going?"

"OK."

She smiled. "What are you doing?"

"Nothing. How was work?"

She shrugged. “Boring.”

Mum has two jobs. She works part-time at the local library, which she likes, and she works part-time at the check-out at Tesco, which she hates. Today was a Tesco day.

She took her hands out of her pockets, crossed her arms, and leaned against the doorway. Her bracelets jangled on her wrists.

“What are you doing tonight?” I asked her.

“Not much. How about you?”

A train juddered along the tracks at the far end of the estate. The bedroom window rattled in its frame.

“I’ve got homework,” I said.

Mum nodded. “I just saw Della’s mum in the lift. She said you hadn’t been round for a while.”

“Right.”

Mum smiled. “Della could do with some company.”

This was Della Hood she was talking about. Della lived on the same floor as us. She was a year younger than me. She had something wrong with her heart.

“She likes you,” Mum said.

I shrugged. I felt a bit embarrassed.

Mum smiled again. "Well, it's up to you. Homework or a pretty young girl? I know which one I'd choose."

"Yeah, well," I muttered, "I'll think about it."

"Have you had anything to eat yet?"

"No."

"Let me get changed," she said, "then I'll make us something – OK?"

I smiled at her.

She nodded, looked at me for a moment, then left.

She's half-Mexican, my mum. She was born in a little farming village in the north of Mexico. She came to England when she was a baby with *her* mum. Just the two of them together. My mum never knew who her father was.

But I know who my father was. His name was David Cherry. He was a policeman, a detective, an officer in the CID. He met my mum about 16 years ago when she was working as a dancer in a nightclub. He was already married. But he fell in love with my mum. They had an affair. And then along came me.

The affair didn't last long. And Dad never left his wife, but he always kept in touch with us. He was great – kind and cool, really funny, but sort of sad, too. I liked him a lot.

Five years ago he was killed in a drug raid.

No one was ever charged or arrested for his murder. The killer was never found.

Maybe that's why I want to be a private detective. Maybe I want to be like my dad. Or maybe I want to find out who killed him. Maybe I just thought it was better than doing a paper round.

Who knows?

I really miss my dad.

CHAPTER 3
MARCUS AND DELLA

After Mum and I had had something to eat, I went to see Della. I wasn't really sure if I *wanted* to see her. But I didn't want to spend all night staring at history books either. I said goodbye to Mum and walked along to Della's flat. I was feeling a bit nervous. Della always made me feel like that. I knew that she liked me, and – to be honest – I quite liked her. But what was a bit difficult was that I didn't really know *how* I liked her. Was she a friend? A good friend? Or did I like her a bit *more* than just as a friend?

I didn't know.

I got to her door and rang the bell. As I waited, I started to see her face in my mind. She had curly blonde hair, sparkling blue eyes, and a brace on her teeth. In my head I could see that funny little smile – and when I heard the sound of footsteps coming towards the door, my heart started thumping. But when the door opened, it wasn't Della that I saw, but her older brother, Marcus.

"Hey, Delgado," he said with a big grin. "What's happening?"

"Oh, right … hi, Marcus. I was looking for Della."

"She's out," he said. "Gone to see the ticker man."

I didn't know what he meant, so I just went on looking at him. He didn't have a shirt on, just big baggy combats and a string of gold chains around his neck. A tufty little beard sprouted from his chin.

"Della's heart," Marcus said, and he gave his chest a slap. "Playing her up a bit today."

"Oh," I said.

I got it now. Della had gone to see her doctor, something to do with her heart.

"Hey, it's cool." Marcus grinned. "She'll be back."

"Right."

"You wanna wait?"

"OK."

And that's how I ended up talking to Marcus about Lee Kirk.

Marcus Hood knows everything there is to know about the estate. He knows all the names and faces, all the gangs, all the goings-on. He knows who's coming up, and who's going down, and who's getting out. He knows who's robbing who, and who's selling what, and who's going to get it. He knows what's going down before it goes down, and he knows what that means. He knows the lot, basically.

But the funny thing is – no one seems to know anything about him. Even though he knows everyone, he doesn't seem to have any friends. He knows everyone's phone number, but no one knows his. He doesn't work, but he's always got plenty of money. And that usually means drugs. But Marcus doesn't do drugs, and he certainly doesn't sell drugs, but he knows all the gangs and the dealers.

It's kind of odd.

There are rumours, of course. Whispers. I've heard the word "grass" once or twice when people have been talking about Marcus, but no one's ever had any proof. And no one's got the guts to find out. It's not worth it. Marcus isn't that hard himself, but he knows a lot of heavy people. And he's owed a lot of favours. So everyone leaves him alone.

Personally, it's never bothered *me* what Marcus does. As long as he's OK with me, why should I care what he does?

And he *was* OK with me.

That evening, he showed me into the front room, sat me down, and asked if I wanted a cup of tea. It might not sound like much, but I didn't expect him to do that for me, and it made me feel pretty good.

While he was in the kitchen, I had a quick look around the flat. It was exactly the same as mine – same layout, same size, same everything. The only difference was, it was a lot messier. It wasn't dirty or anything, but the whole place was jam-packed with stuff. Everywhere I looked, there were boxes and bags full of all kinds of stuff – computer games, DVDs, CDs, hair-dryers, boxes of perfume and aftershave, piles of brand new clothes. There was even a big cardboard box full of Harry Potter figures sitting on the top of the TV.

Marcus came back in, handed me a mug of tea, then sat down cross-legged on the floor. He'd put a hoodie on. The zip was undone, but the hood was up. He lit a cigarette.

"I hear you've been talking to Carly," he said.

"What?"

"Carly and Bex." He winked at me. "Nice girls."

"Oh, yeah ... right."

He grinned. "You're really doing this P.I. thing then?"

"Sorry?" I asked. I didn't understand.

"P.I. ... private investigator ... private detective ... whatever ... you're really doing it?"

"Yeah, I suppose ..."

He gulped some tea. "Toog told me you found his cat."

I smiled. Marcus was talking about Benny Toogood. Everyone calls him Toog. He's a strange man – six foot six and a real giant. He's got a huge square head and hands like shovels. He's also kind of slow, and not too smart. He's not backward or anything, just very ... *very* ... slow. A few weeks ago, I'd bumped into him in the lift. He was crying. He'd lost his cat, he told me, and he really loved his cat. So I helped him to look for it. And I found it. It was at the vet's. Toog had taken it in that morning to get its nails clipped, and then he'd simply forgotten all about it.

"You're his hero," Marcus told me. "Toog thinks you're a genius."

"Toog's all right," I said.

"Yeah," Marcus agreed. "He's cool." He took a long drag on his cigarette. Then he looked at me. "You never know when you might need someone like Toog," he said. "It's always good to have someone looking out for you." He tapped his cigarette into an ashtray. "Most of all if you're stupid enough to get mixed up with people like Lee Kirk." He looked at me again. "You know who he is, don't you?" he asked.

I shrugged. "Sort of ..."

Marcus shook his head. “He’s The Man, that’s who he is. Or he soon will be.”

For the next ten minutes, Marcus told me all about Lee Kirk. He told me how he’d worked himself up from being a simple gang member to being second-in-command of the Westies, the gang who run the West Tower, and that he was now getting ready to take out the current boss, a kid called Tyrell Jones, and then take control of the Westies himself. After that, he planned to join up with the other local gang, the E Boys, and take over the whole estate.

“Kirk’s a psycho,” Marcus told me. “But he’s clever, too. Very clever. He knows how it works, all the gang stuff – the rules, the drugs, the guns. He knows how to play it. Do you know what I mean?”

“Not really,” I said.

Marcus laughed. “Yeah, well, that’s good. Keep it that way and you’ll be all right. Don’t get sucked into it, man. The whole gang thing is a load of shit. It’s a cop-out. They think it’s all about power and money, which it is, but they don’t *use* it for anything. They just hang around, wasting time, talking shit, waiting for something to happen.” He looked at me. “But listen – Kirk’s different. He’s ambitious. He’s going places. And if anyone gets in his way, he won’t think twice about taking him out. So, be careful – OK?”

"I'm only going to follow him. He won't even know I'm there."

Marcus shook his head. "He'll know."

"Yeah, well ..."

Marcus shrugged. "It's up to you. I'm just letting you know, that's all."

"Yeah ... thanks."

The room went quiet for a while, and everything felt kind of edgy. Marcus kept looking right at me for a moment. He gave me a long, hard look. Then slowly, and without a smile, he finished drinking his tea and stood up. He scratched his belly, yawned, then grinned at me.

"All right?"

"Yeah."

"OK."

With that, Marcus strode over to the TV and cracked open the big cardboard box that was sitting on the top. The next thing I knew, Marcus was offering me a Harry Potter figure in a plastic box.

"You want a Hagrid?" he said

"That's Snape," I told him.

He shrugged. "Whatever – you want it?"

"No, thanks."

"Suit yourself."

Just then, the door opened and Della came in with her mum. Della didn't look very well. Her face was pale and tired, and there was a small Band-Aid on her neck. Her mum was carrying a big bottle of pills and an oxygen mask.

I stood up.

Della smiled at me. "Hello, Johnny."

"Hey," I said. "How's it going?"

"I'm all right. I was just –"

"Della," her mum cut in, "you get off to bed now."

"Can't I just –?"

"Not now." Mrs Hood looked at me, then back at Della. "You can see Johnny some other time. Right now you need to get some rest. Go on."

Della gave me an awkward smile. I smiled back at her. She gave me a little wave, then turned round and went off to her room. I looked quickly over at Mrs Hood. She looked worried. I looked down. I felt a bit embarrassed. Like I was an intruder or something.

"I'd better go," I mumbled.

Mrs Hood just nodded silently and went into the kitchen. I watched her go. She looked sad and very tired. The sadness seemed to stay in the air behind her like a poisonous cloud.

Marcus stood up and put his hand on my shoulder. "Hey, don't worry about it," he told me. "Mum just gets worked up about things. Next time you see her she'll be fine."

I looked at him.

He smiled. "Don't *worry*. I'll tell Della you'll call her in a couple of days. She'll be fine by then. OK?"

"Yeah, OK," I said.

"Right." He grinned. "Go on then, piss off home. I got stuff to do." He patted me on the shoulder. "And don't forget what I said about Kirk. Just watch yourself – OK?"

CHAPTER 4
THINKING AND WAITING

I spent most of Saturday just hanging around the flat doing nothing. Mum was working at the library today. And I was on my own.

So I was thinking.

Mostly, I was thinking about Lee Kirk.

I kept looking at his photo, the one that Carly had given me. And every time I looked at it, I thought about what Marcus had said. "He's a psycho ... he's clever ... he's different ... be careful." The more I thought about it, the more I wanted to get in touch with Carly and tell her I'd changed my mind. I didn't want to go snooping around after a psycho. It was stupid. Dangerous. Scary. But I'd said I'd do it, hadn't I? I'd taken the money. And if I really wanted to be a private detective, I couldn't change my mind about a job just because I'd got a bit scared, could I?

That wouldn't be right.

I'd said I'd do it, so I'd do it.

Anyway, I didn't know how to get in touch with Carly. I hadn't got her address or phone number. She'd said she would phone me to see what I'd found out.

Stupid.

At 6.30 that evening, just after Mum got home, I put on my coat, picked up my phone, and got ready to leave.

"Going out?" said Mum.

"Yeah, I won't be long."

"Where are you going?"

"Steve's place."

"Steve who?"

"Steve Devine. You know, from school? He lives in the West Tower."

Mum shrugged, as if she'd never heard of Steve Devine. That wasn't surprising. I'd just made him up.

"All right," she said. "Well, mind how you go. And don't be too late."

There are three tower blocks on the estate – the North Tower (mine), the West Tower, and the East Tower.

Each of them has 23 floors, and each of the floors has ten flats. 230 flats to a block, nearly 700 flats in all. That's a lot of flats, a lot of people. Each of the floors in each of the blocks is exactly the same. There's a corridor on each floor with a row of flats on both sides. There's a lift at one end of the corridor and stairs at the other. The doors to the stairwells are dirty yellow. The walls are painted a horrible sickly green, and the floors are covered with some kind of dirty brown plasticky stuff. There are lights in the ceiling, a couple of windows at the end of each corridor, and that's about it.

There was no one around when I left my flat. The corridor was empty, the lift was empty. When I got out downstairs, there was no one there either.

I headed off across towards the West Tower. The space in between the towers is called "the square" ... I don't know why it's called that. It isn't a square. It's just a rough patch of tarmac with a few crappy benches and a road at one end. It's not even a square *shape*.

The road goes in between the North Tower and the other two towers and I headed across it. The evening light was beginning to dim, and a fine rain was falling. I could hear loud music blaring out from a flat somewhere, but there were hardly any people around. A homeless old guy was digging through the bins by the benches, and there were a couple of E Boys hanging around on the other side of the road, but that was about it.

I crossed the road and hurried over to the West Tower. It was getting cold now. The clouds were low and heavy, and an icy wind was whipping around the estate, blowing rain into my face. In the cold shadows of the tower blocks, everything looked dark and gloomy.

I gazed up. The West Tower was in front of me, the East was to my left, and the North was behind me. Three great blocks of dirty grey concrete, 700 poky little flats, 2000 or so people.

It's a world within a world.

As I came up to the entrance of the West Tower, I saw a few younger kids hanging around the doors. Most of them were on bikes, and most of them had mobile phones. They were runners. Delivery boys. Look-outs. Working for the Westies. The oldest of them was about 12 years old. They watched me as I went through the doors and into the downstairs lobby. One of them came over and stood next to me as I pressed the button for the lift. He had chains around his neck and a snotty nose.

When the lift came down, the snotty kid got in with me.

"What floor d'you want?" he said.

"Thirteen," I lied.

He hit the buttons – 13 and 18.

The doors closed and the lift started moving. I looked at the kid. He stared at the phone in his hand. It was a top-of-the-range Nokia – camera, games, movies, everything.

When the lift stopped at 13 and I stepped out, I saw the kid put the phone to his ear and start talking. I waited for the doors to close, then I went down the corridor and walked up the stairs to the 14th. I didn't open the stairwell doors and go into the corridor yet.

It was five to seven.

I stood in the stairwell and waited.

CHAPTER 5
EVERYTHING GOES BLACK

From where I was standing, I couldn't see the door to Lee Kirk's flat, but I thought I'd hear him when he came out. And I was right. Bang on seven o'clock, I heard a door open, and when I opened the stairwell door and stepped out into the corridor, there he was – Lee Kirk. Coming out of his flat. His blond hair was all gelled up, and he was wearing black joggers and a white Nike hoodie.

He wasn't very big, but he looked a lot nastier than his photograph. Nasty and cold and hard.

My heart was pounding as I walked along the corridor towards him. I pulled a piece of paper from my pocket and pretended to read it. Earlier, I'd written a name and address on the paper, a made-up name and address – "Barry Jennings, Flat 1604, West Tower, William B. Foster Estate." The idea was that if anyone asked me what I was doing here, I could pretend I was lost. I was just some dopey kid, looking for someone called Barry Jennings. It wasn't much of an idea, but it was better than nothing.

And Lee Kirk wasn't even looking at me anyway. As I walked past him, frowning at my piece of paper, he was too busy locking his door and sorting out his phone and stuff to notice me.

So far, so good.

I carried on down to the end of the corridor and stopped by the lift. I waited, pretending to study my piece of paper again. When I heard Kirk's footsteps coming up behind me, I hit the button for the lift. The light came on, and I heard the distant whirring and clunking of the lift as it started moving up the shaft.

I could sense Kirk standing behind me now. I could smell his aftershave. I could feel his presence. It didn't feel good. I forced myself to stay calm. *Don't move, don't turn round, don't look at him.*

The lift seemed to take an age.

I was beginning to sweat.

My legs felt shaky.

The silence was killing me.

I wanted to turn round and say – "Hi, I'm not following you, you know. Honestly. I'm not doing anything. I'm just waiting for the lift ..."

But I forced myself not to.

In the end, after the longest 30 seconds of my life, I heard a dull-sounding *ting*, and then a juddering *clunk* as the lift finally arrived.

I stared at the doors, waiting for them to open.

And when they did, that's when everything went wrong.

There were two of them in the lift. A tall kid in wrap-around shades, and an ugly-looking guy with a face like a pizza. The pizza-faced guy had a bottle in his hand. They were both staring at me.

I didn't even have time to step back. As soon as the doors opened, Kirk grabbed me from behind and shoved me into the lift, and before I knew what was happening, someone hit me hard in the belly and I fell to the floor, gasping for breath.

"Doors," I heard someone say.

A button thumped, and I heard the doors closing. As the lift started moving, I tried to get to my feet, but I didn't have a chance. The first kick slammed me back to the floor, the second one got me in the belly again, and the third one made everything go black.

CHAPTER 6
THE FALL

I'm floating in space. Everything's dark. Stars are spinning faintly in the distance. There are planets, big square planets. Square and flat, like walls. Silver walls. Wooden walls. They keep drifting towards me, knocking into my head, then bouncing away. They're ships. I'm drowning. I'm drinking the sea. It tastes sweet. Sweet and strong. Sour and fruity. It's black ...

Everything's black.

Everything's gone.

When I woke up, the first thing I saw was that I was holding a knife. A big, heavy knife. The silver blade was sticky with blood. My hand was red, too. I opened my fingers and the knife fell to the floor.

The floor was grey. A grey carpet.

My head hurt.

My belly hurt.

I felt sick.

I couldn't remember anything.

I closed my eyes and tried to think – *Where am I? What happened to me? Where did the knife come from? Why is it covered in blood?*

Nothing. No answers. My mind was empty. I could remember Kirk shoving me into the lift, then someone kicking me in the head ... but that was it. After that – nothing.

I opened my eyes and looked around.

I was lying on a grubby settee in the front room of a dim and shadowy flat. The curtains were shut. It was dark outside. Night-time. Late. The TV was on, *Match of the Day*, the sound turned off. The room was a mess – unwashed plates on the table, dirty clothes on the floor, rubbish all over the place. The air smelled stale. The flat felt empty and quiet, but I could hear dim sounds from somewhere else – rap music, voices shouting, a police car wailing in the distance.

The sounds of the estate.

'I'm still on the estate,' I thought. 'I'm in a flat, somewhere on the estate.'

It didn't make me feel much better, but at least it was something. I felt in my pocket for my phone, but it wasn't there. I searched all my other pockets –

nothing. I started to sit up, groaning at the pain in my belly ... and that's when I saw him.

He was lying on the floor by the window. Face up, his eyes wide open, staring at nothing. He was covered in blood.

It was Tyrell Jones, the leader of the Westies.

I knew he was dead, but I still had to check. My legs felt wobbly as I went over and crouched down beside him. When I saw all the blood, I thought I was going to be sick. He'd been stabbed in the chest and the stomach. I could see the stab wounds through his shirt – deep and ugly, thick with blood. There were at least three of them, maybe more. His hands were cut, too. And his face was all battered and smashed.

I put my fingers on his neck and felt for his pulse, but there was nothing.

He wasn't breathing.

His skin was cold.

He was dead.

Stabbed ...

I looked down at the blood on my hands. There was blood on my shirt, too. But I wasn't hurt. It wasn't my blood. My heart sank as I looked over at the knife I'd dropped on the floor ... the knife I'd had in my hand when I woke up.

The knife …

I looked back at Tyrell's body again. The stab wounds in his chest …

Then I looked at the knife.

The stab wounds.

The knife.

Oh, God … had *I* killed him?

Had I stabbed Tyrell Jones to death?

My head was spinning now. I was trying to think, trying to remember, trying to stay calm. But I couldn't. Couldn't think. Couldn't remember. Couldn't stay calm.

I couldn't do anything. All I could do was stare at the blood on my hands.

Then I heard it again – the police siren. It was closer now. A *lot* closer. I got to my feet fast and went over to the window. I heard the sound of tyres squealing outside, and when I pulled back the curtain I saw the flashing lights of two patrol cars swerving off the road and speeding into the estate.

I closed the curtain.

Which tower was I in?

Breathing fast, I opened the curtain again, took a quick look around outside, then shut it again.

I was in the West Tower. Third or fourth floor.

I was in a lot of trouble.

I was trapped in a room with a dead body. I had blood on my hands, and my fingerprints were all over the murder weapon. The police would be here any minute, and I couldn't explain anything. I didn't even know how I'd got here.

I had to get out.

I tried the front door, but it was locked. No key. I ran back into the front room and looked out of the window again. The police cars were parked down below. Their doors were shut but the lights were still flashing. Kids from the estate were beginning to crowd the cars, laughing and shouting. I guessed the policemen must be on their way up now. Some in the lift, some on the stairs. Covering all exits.

I leaned out of the window now and looked straight down. I could see the window of the flat below. It was open. Could I get down there? The outside wall was smooth, but halfway down, between me and the flat below, there was a ventilation shaft. If I could just get a foothold on that ...

I didn't have time to think. I could hear running footsteps in the corridor now. Voices. Police radios.

I opened the window and crawled out onto the sill ...

Fists started hammering on the door.

I grabbed hold of the window sill and let my legs slide down ...

Shouts – "Police! Open up! Open the door!"

My feet couldn't find the ventilation shaft. I was hanging on the sill, three floors up, waving my feet around in the air.

THUMP! The front door of the flat cracked and splintered. They'd kicked it in ... I took a deep breath, closed my eyes, and let go of the ledge. For a terrifying instant, I just fell – my heart frozen, my hands scrabbling madly at the wall – and then my feet hit the ventilation shaft. I felt it crack, then my feet started to slip off, and for a moment I was falling again. Somehow I grabbed hold of a bit of the ventilation shaft as I fell, and at the same time my feet struck the window ledge of the flat below. The next thing I knew I was scrambling in through the open window and dropping down onto the floor.

Above me, I could hear a door smash open and heavy boots crashing into the room.

I shut the window and breathed out hard.

I was shaking like a wreck.

CHAPTER 7
MADNESS AND GOODNESS

"Can I help you?"

The voice came from the middle of the room behind me. I spun round and saw a mad-looking old woman standing there. My mouth dropped open. I'd totally forgotten that someone might *live* in the flat I'd fallen into. I was too shocked to speak. I just stood there and stared, and the woman stared back at me.

She was about a million years old. Her hair was wild and grey, like a mad bird's nest, and her wrinkly old face was covered in make-up – purple eyes, jet-black eyebrows, bright pink lips. She was wearing a blue tracksuit, cheap white trainers, and a pair of black lace gloves.

Mad as a bat.

"I know you," she said suddenly.

"Sorry?"

"You're Maria's boy, aren't you? Jimmy Delgado."

"Johnny," I said.

She cupped a hand to her ear. "What?"

"Johnny ... Johnny Delgado."

"That's what I said." She clacked her teeth. "Your mum's a kind lady. She helped me up the stairs once. She told me all about you, said you were a good boy."

"Right ..."

I could hear more sirens now. More police. I could hear them upstairs, in the corridor, knocking on all the other doors.

"Betty Travis," the old woman said.

"What?"

"My name's Betty Travis. I expect your mum told you about me. She helped me up the stairs, you know."

"Yeah ..."

"What have you done?" she said.

"Sorry?"

She stared at me. "I might be a bit mad, young man, but I'm not stupid. You've just climbed through my window. The police are all over the place. You're sweating and shaking and you're covered in blood." She smiled at me. "If you want me to help you, I think you'd better start talking."

I thought about running for it, just legging it out of the door, but I knew I wouldn't get very far. Betty was right – I needed help. I didn't know *why* she wanted to help me, and I didn't know *how* she could help me, but there was nothing else I could do.

So I started talking.

When I'd told her everything I could, she didn't say anything for a while, just stared at me.

After what seemed like a long time, she said, "Do you expect me to believe all that?"

I shrugged. "It's the truth."

She looked at me for a moment longer, then nodded. "Right," she said. "The bathroom's down there. Get yourself washed and out of those clothes."

Five minutes later, I was pushing Betty down the corridor to the lift in a wheelchair. My hands were clean, the blood was washed off, and I had a scratchy blue tracksuit on. My own blood-stained clothes were tumbling around in Betty's washing machine.

As we got nearer to the lift, I saw there were two policeman standing guard beside it.

"Keep your mouth shut," Betty whispered. "Let me do the talking."

I carried on wheeling her towards the lift. The two policemen were watching us now. I tried to look as innocent as possible. I was just some kid … a kid with a batty old gran in a wheelchair. That's all I was.

We were almost at the lift, when suddenly Betty started to shake her head to and fro and jabber away like a mad woman. "What's going on?" she cackled. "What's this?" She waved her hands at the policemen. "Who are you? What do you want? I haven't done anything … what's going on?"

Both the policemen looked startled. They turned to me.

"Sorry," I said, "she's just a bit –"

"Jimmy?" Betty screeched. "Jimmy … what's this? What do they want? I haven't done anything …"

One of the policemen pressed the lift button. The other one tried to smile. It was the kind of smile you give to mad people.

While Betty carried on jabbering and screeching, I smiled back at the policeman. "What's going on?" I asked him in a casual voice. "Has there been some trouble?"

He shrugged. "Nothing to worry about."

I nodded.

Betty lurched forward and swung her arm at him.

I pulled her back into the wheelchair. "Sorry …"

The lift doors opened, and the policemen moved to one side. I wheeled Betty into the lift and hit the button for the ground floor. Betty kept on with her crazy act until the doors had closed again and the lift had started moving, and then she suddenly stopped.

"All right?" she said calmly and smiled at me.

"Very good," I said. "Very realistic."

She laughed. "I've had a lot of practice."

There were more police downstairs, and more outside the tower block, but none of them bothered us. Maybe the others had radioed down to let them know we were coming. Most of the estate kids hanging around outside were too busy jumping round the patrol cars to notice me, but I saw one or two of them nudge each other and point at me. But no one said anything.

I wheeled Betty across the road, through the square, and into the North Tower. I couldn't see any policemen around yet, but I was pretty sure they'd be here soon, so I didn't waste any time. Into the lobby, into the lift, shut the doors.

"Tenth floor," Betty said.

"What?"

"I've got a friend on the tenth floor. You can drop me off there."

I hit 10.

The lift started moving.

I looked down at Betty. "Why are you doing this?" I asked her. "Why are you helping me?"

"Your eyes," she said.

"My eyes?"

She smiled at me. "You have good eyes."

Tenth floor. The doors opened and Betty got out. She pushed the wheelchair out in front of her.

"Thank you," I said.

She smiled again. "Come and see me some time. Keep a mad woman company for a while."

"OK," I said.

She put her hand into the pocket of her tracksuit and passed me a mobile phone. "Here, take it. Let your mum know you're all right. You can bring it back when you come round to see me." She leaned back into the lift and pressed the button for the 23rd floor. Then she stepped back. "*Adios*, Johnny," she said.

As the doors shut I stared at her, unable to speak.

How did she know I needed a phone? And how did she know I was going to the 23rd floor?

How did she *know* that? It's not as if it's where I live.

CHAPTER 8
SECRETS AND LIES

I've got a secret hiding place.

To get to it, you have to go up to the 23rd floor and follow the corridor right down to the end. Then you go through a door marked – PRIVATE. NO ENTRY! The door is always locked, so you need a key. I've had my key for about three years now. I borrowed it from the man from the council. He left the key in the door by mistake. I keep my key hidden away beneath a piece of loose floor near the door.

I go to my secret place when I want to be on my own and think about things. And that night I really needed to be on my own and think about things. There was a lot to think about.

After I'd made sure that no one was watching me, I got the key from under the flooring, opened the door, then locked it behind me. The door goes into a little room that's filled with all sorts of stuff – cupboards and shelves, boxes of tools, pipes and cables, heating controls. I went across the room and through a little archway. Then I went up some steps to another door. I pushed open that door and stepped out into a breeze of cold night air. I was on the roof of the tower block now. High above the ground. I could see for miles. I could see the lights of houses and blocks of flats, headlights streaming on invisible roads, street lights, traffic lights, the lights of London glowing in the distance.

But there wasn't time to enjoy the view.

I hurried across the roof, heading towards my secret place.

My secret place is a shed. A metal shed. It has a metal door, metal walls, and a metal roof. Inside, there's a big metal cabinet covered in dials and displays. I'm not sure what it is, but it hums all the time. It's also nice and warm. Apart from the cabinet and a couple of old chairs, the rest of the shed is empty.

Empty and quiet. I shut the door behind me, sat down on one of the chairs, and started to think.

Think.

What's going on?

What happened?

How?

Why?

What are you going to do?

I thought about it. I thought hard, looking for why everything had happened the way it did. Looking for answers. Looking for facts. I tried to remember ... but I still couldn't. My head felt thick and dizzy.

I decided to stick to the facts.

Fact 1 – Someone had killed Tyrell Jones.

Fact 2 – Either that someone was me, or someone else had framed me. They'd made it look as if it was me.

Fact 3 – Even if I could kill someone, which I didn't think I could, why would I kill Tyrell Jones?

Fact 4 – Lee Kirk wanted to kill Tyrell Jones. If Marcus was right, and most of the time he is right, Kirk was planning to take over all the gangs on the estate. With Tyrell out of the way, there was nothing to stop him.

Fact 5 – Kirk was a psycho.

Fact 6 – Kirk was clever.

What did it all add up to? Kirk had set me up. He'd got Carly and Bex to hire me so that I'd follow him. Then he'd got me in the lift, beaten me up and left me in the flat with Tyrell's dead body. Maybe he'd called the police, too. Had he given them my name as well?

Why? So that no one would know who the real killer was. And the real killer was him. Kirk.

Yeah, but why did Kirk choose me? Why did I have to take the rap?

I didn't know the answer to that. Right now that didn't matter. What was bothering me right now was – what the hell was I going to do?

I called Mum first. I got Betty's mobile out of my pocket, put in the number, and waited.

"Hello?"

"Mum, it's me –"

"*Hola, Juan. Cómo estás?*"

"What?" I said. "It's me, Mum – Johnny. Why are you speaking Spanish?"

"*Policía,*" she whispered. "*Dónde estás?*"

I got it then. She was speaking Spanish because the police were there. In the flat. She didn't want them to know she was talking to me. She wanted to know where I was.

"*Estoy a salvo,*" I told her. (I'm safe.) "*No he hecho nada.*" (I haven't done anything.)

"*Ya lo sé*," she said. (I know.) "*No vengas a casa todavía. Llama a Della – OK*?" (Don't come home yet. Call Della – OK?)

"OK," I said.

She put her phone down.

I thought about what she'd just said for a moment, then I called Della.

"Hello?"

"Della – it's Johnny."

"Johnny!" she cried. "What's going on? Are you all right? I was with your mum just now and the police came round. They're looking for you."

"Yeah, I know. I just spoke to Mum on the phone."

"Where are you? All you all right?"

"I'm fine. What did the police say?"

"They wanted to know where you were. They wouldn't say why." She hesitated a moment. "They found the letter, Johnny."

"What letter?"

"It was hidden in the bathroom."

"*What?* What are you *talking* about?"

"One of the policemen went into your bathroom and came back with a letter. I only saw it for a second. It was something to do with your dad."

"My dad?" I couldn't believe it. "A letter about my *dad*?"

"Yeah ... haven't you seen it?"

"I don't know anything about any letter. What did it say?"

Della hesitated again. "It didn't say who it was from ... it wasn't signed ..."

"But what did it *say*, Della?"

"Whoever wrote it ... they said they knew who killed your dad. They named him."

I couldn't speak for a moment. I was too confused. Too shocked.

"Johnny?" said Della. "Are you still there?"

"Who did it?" I said quietly. "Who killed my dad?"

"Someone called Jones," Della said. "Lester Jones."

It was too much. Everything was just too much.

My mind went blank and I stared at the floor.

Lester Jones was Tyrell Jones's father.

CHAPTER 9
SOMETHING AND NOTHING

"Johnny? Yo, Johnny D! You there? Hey, Delgado? Hey? *HEY* ... speak to me."

The voice on the phone seemed miles away. I was miles away. My mind was still blank.

I couldn't think.

The voice called out again. "Hey! HEY! *HEY!*"

Still in a daze, I lifted my hand from my lap and put the phone to my ear. "Hello?"

"Delgado? Christ, what are you *doing*? I thought you'd *died* or something."

It was Marcus.

"Sorry ..." I mumbled. "I was just thinking ..."

"You ain't got time to think. You're up to your neck in shit. I *told* you not to go messing with Kirk."

"Yeah ..."

"All right, listen," he said. "You listening?"

"Yeah."

"Right, talk to me. Tell me what happened."

I told Marcus everything. From getting beaten up in the lift, to wheeling Betty Travis out of the West Tower and across to the North, then talking to Mum and Della on the phone. Everything. When I'd finished, Marcus was quiet for a second or two, and I imagined him sitting in his flat with the phone to his ear, thinking hard.

"OK," he said after a while. "I think I get it."

"Kirk set me up," I said.

"Of *course* he did," Marcus said with a sigh. "I knew that before I even spoke to you. I just didn't know how he did it."

"Do you know now?"

"The guy in the lift ... you said he was carrying a bottle?"

"Yeah."

"They drugged you. After they'd beaten you up, they made you drink whatever was in the bottle. It was probably full of roofies or something."

"What are roofies?"

"You know, they're the date-rape drug. Roofies make you feel drunk and sleepy, and when you wake up you can't remember anything. They drugged you, killed Tyrell, then left you in his flat with the knife they'd used to murder Tyrell. Then they called the cops."

"What about the letter they found in the bathroom?" I asked him. "I don't understand –"

"It's a fake," he said. "Kirk probably wrote it. Carly and Bex planted it when they were at your place."

"Why?"

"It gives you a reason for killing Tyrell. You get a letter saying his dad killed your dad, you've got a reason to kill him."

"That's *crazy*. I wouldn't –"

"It worked, didn't it?" Marcus said. "The police are looking for you. They're not looking for Kirk, are they?"

He was right, of course. I could see it all now. Marcus was right. He'd been right all along. And I'd been even stupider than I thought.

"Where are you now?" Marcus said.

"On the roof. You go up to the top floor –"

"Yeah, I know how to get there. Are you in the shed?"

"How do *you* know about the shed?"

He laughed. "I know everything."

"Yeah, but –"

"Just stay there, OK? I'll be with you in about 20 minutes."

"What are you going to do?"

"You'll find out when I get there," he said.

It was a long 20 minutes. I sat in the shed for a while, just trying to think, but there was too much going on in my head. Too many feelings, too many emotions.

Fear.

Anger.

Shame.

Sadness.

When Della had told me about the letter, I'd felt something stir inside me. The idea that Lester Jones had killed my dad ... well, it was something. Something to hold on to. A name, at last. A suspect. Someone to blame.

But now, now that I knew it wasn't true ...

Now there was nothing again.

I stopped thinking and went out onto the roof.

The night air was really cold now. Cold and fresh and silent. The sky was pitch black, and the world stretched out beneath me. Twenty-three floors below. I stood on the edge of the roof and looked down. In the glow of the flashing blue lights, I could see the dim outline of the square. The lock-up garages. The bins. The benches.

Twenty-three floors below.

It was a long way down.

CHAPTER 10
HOW DO YOU THINK IT FEELS?

When the door to the roof opened, I was surprised to see that Marcus wasn't alone. I was even more surprised when I saw who was with him. As he came through the door, I saw the giant figure of Toog behind him. And behind Toog, being dragged by his hair, was Lee Kirk.

"Hey, Johnny," Marcus said, "how's it going?"

I looked at Toog. He grinned at me. He was dragging Lee Kirk in one huge hand, almost lifting him off his feet. Kirk was squirming and twisting around, gripping Toog's hand to stop his hair being pulled out by the roots. His nose was bleeding and one of his eyes was black and blue and swollen.

The three of them came over to me, and we stood there together at the edge of the roof. I put my hand in my pocket and felt for Betty's phone.

"What's going on?" I asked Marcus.

"Not much," he said. "I just thought it was time we had a little chat with The Man here. You know, get things sorted ..." He glanced at Kirk. "What do you think, Lee? You feel like talking?"

Kirk glared at him. "You're a dead man, Hood. You're finished –"

"Yeah, yeah," Marcus said calmly. "You've already told me all that. It's getting kind of boring. How about telling us something else?"

"Like what?"

"Like how you set Johnny up, for a start."

Kirk spat on the floor, then grinned coldly at me. "How's your head, kid? You look a bit pale." He laughed. "Hey, I hear you found out who killed your old man. Is that right?"

I stared at him.

"Lester Jones, eh?" He laughed again. "Who'd have thought it? I knew all those rumours weren't true."

"What rumours?" I said.

Kirk looked at Marcus. "Doesn't he know?"

"Shut up, Kirk," Marcus said.

Kirk ignored him, turning back to me with a grin. "Your old man … they say he was taken out by another cop. A contract hit." He raised his eyebrows. He thought it was funny that I was so shocked. "Didn't you know? I thought everyone on the estate knew that."

I looked at Marcus. "What's he talking about?"

"Nothing," Marcus said quickly. "Don't listen to him. He's just trying to wind you up." He turned to Kirk, his eyes suddenly hard. "You talk too much."

"Yeah? What are you going to do about it?"

"How about I throw you off the roof?"

Kirk shook his head. "If you think you can scare me –"

"I'm not trying to scare you," Marcus said simply. "I'm just going to kill you." He glanced up at Toog. "Ready?"

Toog nodded.

"Do it," Marcus told him.

Toog raised his hand and started dragging Kirk towards the edge of the roof. For a moment or two, Kirk didn't do anything. He didn't believe they were serious. He thought they were just bluffing. But as Toog dragged him ever closer to the edge, Kirk began to see that maybe they *weren't* bluffing after all, and that's when he started to panic.

"Hey ... hold on," he shouted, "come on, don't be stupid ... no, you can't ... hey, lemme go ..."

He was digging his heels in now, struggling hard. His eyes were white with fear as he tried to free himself from Toog's giant hand. But Toog was too strong. He didn't even wait, just pulled Kirk right up to the edge of the roof, then grabbed him with both hands and lifted him off his feet ...

And I thought that was it.

I really thought he was going to throw Kirk off.

And maybe he would have.

But just as he lifted him up, the door to the roof slammed open, and we all turned round to see who it was.

It was Della. She was breathing heavily and her face was sickly white. She was clutching a hand to her chest.

"Della!" cried Marcus. "What the hell ...? I *told* you to stay at home."

"I was worried," she gasped. She looked over at me. "I just wanted to –"

Thump.

The sudden sound came from behind me.

I turned round and saw Toog crashing to the ground. We'd all taken our eyes off Kirk for a moment. And while we weren't watching him, he'd head-butted Toog and knocked him out. And now Kirk was going after Marcus.

"Marcus!" I yelled.

But I was too late. As Marcus turned round, Kirk flashed past me and laid Marcus out with a brutal punch to the head. I was too shocked to move. All I could do was stand there and watch as Kirk kicked Marcus in the head. Then he turned round and started running for the door.

Della was too shocked to move, too. She was still standing in front of the door. Just standing there, staring at Kirk. He was running right at her.

"Della!" I shouted. "Move! Get out of the way!"

When she heard me screech at her like that, she moved – a fearful step to one side. But it didn't do her any good. Because Kirk wasn't running for the door, after all – he was running for her. I watched in horror as he swerved to one side and grabbed her by the hand. Then he started dragging her back across the roof towards me.

I looked around. Marcus was still out of it, groaning quietly on the ground, and Toog was just lying there like a fallen tree. I looked back at Kirk and Della.

Della was grasping her chest. She could hardly breathe.

Kirk was grinning at me.

"Leave her alone," I told him. "She's got nothing to do with this."

His grin got even bigger.

"She's sick," I said. "She's got a bad heart."

"Yeah? That's a shame."

He jerked her hand. She stumbled and yelped. He dragged her to her feet and put his arm round her neck, then pushed her over to the edge of the roof. His eyes were shining with madness now. He was crazy. Grinning like a lunatic.

"Fresh air," he shouted at me. "That's what you need when you're sick – plenty of fresh air." He leaned out over the edge and looked down, forcing Della to look down, too. She screamed. Kirk smiled madly at her, then looked at me. "How d'you think it feels?" he yelled. "You know, when you're falling ... plunging down to the ground – how d'you think it feels? D'you think you *think* about anything? What d'you think, Delgado? What would *you* think about?"

I didn't say anything. There wasn't anything to say. I kept my eyes fixed on Della. She was trembling and shaking in Kirk's grip, but I could see she was still in control of herself.

Kirk laughed. "Hey, d'you know what Tyrell said when I stabbed him? D'you know what he said? He said I was making a big mistake. Can you believe that? He's lying there with a knife in his guts, and he says I'm making a big mistake."

Della winked at me.

What was she trying to tell me?

"See," said Kirk, "the trouble with Tyrell was –"

Della suddenly gasped, a loud painful gasp. Then she grabbed at her chest and went limp. Kirk didn't know what to do next. He looked down at Della, slumped in his arms. Just for one moment he stepped back from her so as to hold her a different way. That was what Della was waiting for. As soon as she felt Kirk's arm relax, she threw back her head and nutted him in the face. Then she lifted her foot up and raked her boot down his shin. As Kirk swore and staggered back, Della spun out of his grip and quickly backed away from him. I reached out and pulled her towards me. Kirk lunged after her, trying to grab her arm, but his foot slipped and he missed. And as he fell over, I shoved him away.

And he lost his balance.

Toppled sideways.

Over the edge of the roof.

I don't know *why* I lunged after him and grabbed his hand – I just did. I wasn't thinking about it. I just saw him going over the edge, and the next thing I knew I was lying face down on the roof, with my head over the edge, and Kirk was swinging in my hand below me.

His face peered up at me – petrified, sick, shocked.

His body was twisting in the air.

"Keep still," I told him. I gritted my teeth. "Just hold on ..."

He was heavy.

Twenty-three floors below, I could see crowds of people looking up, their tiny faces lit up in the eerie flashing blue lights from the police cars.

It was a long way down.

"Don't let go," Kirk whimpered. "Please ... don't drop me ..."

I looked at him. I felt strangely calm now. My arm was being pulled out of its socket, and my hand was throbbing, but my head was as clear as a bell.

"Why did you set me up?" I said.

"What?" he hissed.

"I can't hold on for ever," I told him. "The quicker you tell me –"

"All right, all *right*," he spluttered. "It was nothing, OK? I just needed someone to take the heat, take the blame for killing Jones. I set you up, OK? I admit it. Now pull me up, please ..."

"Why me?" I said. "Why choose me?"

"No *reason*," he spat. "I just heard about you, that's all. You know – the private detective kid. You were easy to set up, that's all it was. You were easy."

He looked down. His eyes rolled with fear.

I could feel his hand slipping out of mine.

I put my other hand into my pocket and took out Betty's phone. I looked at the display. The line was still open.

I put the phone to my ear. "Did you get all that?"

"This is the emergency services," a voice said. "Who is this please?"

"My name's Johnny Delgado. I'm on the roof of the North Tower on the William B. Foster estate. Is this call being recorded?"

"Please stay where you are. The police are on their way. Is anybody injured, Johnny? It sounded like –"

I held the phone out to Kirk. "It's been on since you got here," I told him. "They heard everything."

"Please," he begged. "Help me ..."

"One more thing," I said.

"No ..."

"Who killed my dad?"

He shook his head. "I don't know. I was just joking about him ... the letter was a fake. I don't know anything. Please ... I don't *know* ..."

"Name," I said. "Give me a name."

"I *can't* ..."

He was crying now. Tears streaming down his face.

"You're slipping, Lee," I told him. "I can't hold on. Last chance ... give me a name."

He stared up at me, his eyes were bulging. His lips shut tight.

Then finally he blurted out a name.

CHAPTER 11
WORKING ON IT

It took a little while, and lots of explaining, but everything turned out all right in the end.

I didn't drop Kirk off the roof. I wasn't strong enough to haul him back up, but I managed to hang on to him until Marcus and Toog were able to give me a hand, and then it was easy. Once we'd got him back on the roof, Toog was all for giving him a good kicking. But, luckily for Kirk, the police arrived just in time. They arrested the lot of us and took us all down to the station.

Six hours later, I was home and free. Thanks to the 999 call I'd made on the roof, the police had heard everything Kirk had said. They'd heard him admit to Tyrell Jones's murder, and they'd heard him admit he'd set me up. It wasn't enough to *prove* I was innocent, but it was enough for them to let me go.

By Monday morning, the police had charged Kirk with the murder of Tyrell Jones. The tall kid and the guy with the face like a pizza were both arrested and charged with planning to commit murder. Carly and Bex were taken to the police station for questioning and arrested for helping Kirk. They were later released on bail.

Marcus and Toog were both released without charge.

As far as I know, Della is fine. She's still not great, but I think she's doing OK. Her mum has banned me from seeing her now, as she thinks I'm bad for her heart, so we haven't had a chance to meet up for a while. But I'm working on it.

And the name? The name that Kirk blurted out as he was hanging over the edge of the roof ... the name of the man who killed my dad? Well, I'm working on that, too. The name Kirk gave me was Taylor – Jack Taylor. So far, all I've managed to find out about him is that he used to be my dad's boss, and that soon after my dad died he left the police and set up his own private detective agency.

It's not much to go on, I know.

But, like I said, I'm working on it.

I'll let you know how I get on.

PART 2:

LIKE FATHER, LIKE SON

CHAPTER 1
IT'S CHRISTMAS TIME

Christmas has never been that great on the William B. Foster estate. For a few years the council put up a Christmas tree in the square, but it always got vandalised, so they don't bother any more. No one hangs any decorations on their doors, because they'd just get stolen. And we haven't had any carol singers round here since a bunch of Young Christians got beaten up and robbed a few years ago.

No, Christmas has never been that great on the William B. Foster estate.

But it's never been as bad as this.

That's what I was thinking that night as I looked down at the estate from the roof of the North Tower. 'It's never been as bad as this,' I was thinking. And maybe it's all my fault.

It was a cold Sunday night in December, a week before Christmas, and I was waiting for my friend,

Marcus Hood. Marcus lives just down the hallway from me, on the 17th floor of the North Tower. I'd rung him earlier and asked him to meet me at nine o'clock. And now here I was, waiting for him to show up.

I looked at my watch – 9.15.

Marcus was late.

I looked down at the estate below. The ground was a long way down, 23 floors, and the night was dark, but I could still see everything that was going on. I could see gangs of kids with hoodies hanging round the square – little kids, big kids, white kids, black kids. I could see the gangs eyeing each other up – the Westies watching the E Boys, the E Boys watching the Westies. I could see people watching from the windows of the other tower blocks – worried faces, excited faces, puzzled faces. I could see the police cars at the end of the street. They were waiting for the trouble to start. I could see everything, flickering in the light of a burning car across the square.

It didn't look good.

"Jesus, it's cold."

The voice came from behind me. Even though I was expecting it, it still made me jump. But when I turned round and saw Marcus coming across the roof towards me, I couldn't help smiling. He was wearing a long black leather coat, fur gloves, a black fur hat with earflaps, and big black Yeti boots.

"Going hunting?" I asked him.

"I've got thin blood," he said. "I feel the cold – all right?"

"Thin blood?"

"Yeah."

I smiled. "Well, it's better than having fat blood, I suppose."

Marcus didn't say anything. He stopped beside me, rubbed his hands together, and looked down over the roof. A fire engine had pulled up beside the police cars now. The firemen were watching the burning car, but they weren't doing anything about it. They weren't stupid. They knew what would happen if they went anywhere near the car. The kids would start hurling bricks and bottles, that's what would happen.

So the firemen were just waiting. Like everyone else. Just waiting to see what happened.

"When do you think it's going to start?" I asked Marcus.

"Pretty soon," he said. "In a few days or so."

"Not tonight?"

He shook his head. "No, nothing's going to happen tonight." He looked down at the estate. "They're all just showing off now. They're letting the other gangs see what they've got. There won't be any of that when the action kicks off. The place will just suddenly explode."

He lit a cigarette and we both stood there in silence. We watched the gangs down below. From up here, the groups of kids looked small and harmless, like restless ants. But I knew they weren't harmless. I'd found that out myself a couple of months ago. They weren't harmless at all.

"What's up, Johnny?" Marcus said to me.

I looked at him. "Nothing, I was just thinking ..."

"About what?"

"I don't know. All this gang stuff, I suppose."

"What about it?"

"Well ... I just can't help thinking that if I hadn't got mixed up with Lee Kirk and Tyrell Jones, none of this would be happening."

"Yeah, it would," Marcus said. "It was always going to happen. Kirk didn't *need* to frame you to get rid of Tyrell, he would've got rid of him anyway. You just happened to be there at the wrong time, that's all."

"Yeah, but –"

“Listen,” Marcus said, “it’s not your fault, OK? It’s just gang stuff – it would have happened whatever you did. And at least you got Kirk put away.”

“Yeah, I suppose ...”

Marcus put his hand on my arm. “You know what your problem is?” he said.

“What?”

“You think too much.” He grinned at me, then thumped me on the arm and pulled his hat down over his ears. “Come on,” he said, “let’s go in. I’m freezing my nuts off out here.”

As we headed over to a metal shed on the other side of the roof, I thought about what Marcus had just said. I knew he was right – it wasn’t my fault. Lee Kirk was in prison for killing Tyrell Jones. They’d run the Westies gang. So now the Westies had lost their leaders and the E Boys were moving in on their territory. It was just gang stuff, that’s all. It *would’ve* happened whatever I’d done.

But I still felt bad about it.

If I hadn’t done this.

If I hadn’t done that.

If I hadn’t been so stupid.

'Yeah,' I said to myself, 'but if you hadn't done anything, if you'd stayed out of it, you'd never have found out about your dad, would you?'

I was right. I wouldn't have found about my dad. And that's what this was all about.

I needed to find out who'd killed my dad.

CHAPTER 2
WHISPERS AND RUMOURS

The metal shed on the tower block roof had been my secret place. It was where I went when I wanted to be on my own, to think about things, to get some peace and quiet. But things changed a few months ago, and the shed's not so secret any more. But it's still a good place to be. It has a metal door, metal walls and a metal roof. Inside, there's a big metal cabinet covered in dials and displays, and a couple of old wooden chairs. I don't know what the cabinet is, but it hums all the time, and it's always nice and warm.

"That's better," said Marcus. He'd taken off his gloves and was warming his hands in front of the cabinet. "I wish we had one of these in our flat," he said. "It's so cold in there, even the rats wear scarves."

He sat down and lit a cigarette.

I went over and sat down next to him.

"So," Marcus said, "what did you want to see me about? Is it Della?"

I shook my head. Della is 14 – four years younger than Marcus, a year younger than me. Della's got something wrong with her heart. She can still have a normal life, but she has to be careful all the time. And she's always having to go to the hospital for check-ups and scans and operations.

We'd always been friends, me and Della, but over the last few weeks we'd started to be more than just friends. Well, we were *trying* to be more than just friends.

Marcus grinned at me. "Are you still banned from seeing her?"

I nodded. "Your mum thinks I'm bad for her heart."

"Yeah, I know. So how come I saw you two together the other night?"

"When?"

"Friday, when Della was supposed to be at the hospital."

"Oh, right," I muttered, "yeah ... Friday night." I shrugged. "That was nothing. We just happened to bump into each other –"

"Yeah?"

I blushed.

Marcus laughed. "It's all right, don't worry. I won't tell Mum. But just be careful, OK? Della's pretty sick. Make sure you look after her."

"Yeah, I will."

He looked hard at me for a moment – he was Della's big brother, after all. Then he smiled again and puffed on his cigarette.

"So," he said, "if it's not Della, what is it?"

"It's my dad," I told him. "I want to talk to you about David Cherry. My dad."

The smile vanished from Marcus's face.

My dad was a policeman, and five years ago he was killed in a drug raid. His killer has never been found. I was only a kid when it happened. My dad wasn't married to my mum. He was married to someone else. He had a wife, Sonia Cherry. He had a home. He had a life I knew nothing about. So when he got killed, I didn't know anything about that, either. But a few months ago, when all this stuff with Lee Kirk was going on, I started to find things out. And one of the things I found out was that Marcus knew more about my dad than I expected.

"You knew, didn't you?" I said to him now.

"Knew what?"

"Who killed my dad. You've known all along."

Marcus puffed on his cigarette for a while, then looked at me. "Are you sure you want to talk about this?"

"He was my dad, Marcus. Whatever else he was, and whatever anyone thought of him, he was my *dad*. I've got a right to know what happened to him. I want to know what happened to him. And if you don't tell me, I'll find someone else who will. The truth's out there somewhere, and I'm going to find it."

Marcus didn't look at me for while. He sat there smoking his cigarette, lost in thought. I didn't say anything. I just kept still and waited. At last, after what seemed like a very long time, Marcus took off his hat, scratched his shaved head, and looked at me again.

"All right," he said softly, "what do you want to know?"

The first thing I asked him about was a man called Jack Taylor. I'd got Taylor's name from Lee Kirk. That was when Kirk's life had been in my hands – really *in my hands* – I was holding onto him over the edge of the roof, 23 floors up. When I'd asked him to tell me who'd killed my dad, and he'd yelled out Jack Taylor's name, I was pretty sure he was telling the truth.

"Jack Taylor and your dad used to work together," Marcus told me. "Taylor was in charge of the Drug Squad, so he was your dad's boss. They used to call him Tinker – as in Tinker Taylor. He's a nasty shit." Marcus put out his cigarette, then went on talking. "Taylor was bent ... corrupt. Everyone knew it. And it wasn't just him, either. Half the Drug Squad was on the take – pay-offs, bribes, thieving."

"Thieving?" I said. "Thieving what?"

"Drugs, of course. They'd do a raid, keep half the gear for themselves, then sell it back to one of the gangs. Then, a few days later, they'd bust *that* gang and sell the gear on to another gang." Marcus shook his head. "Taylor and his crew just about ran the whole estate. And they were making big money, too."

"What about my dad?" I asked. "Was he involved in all this?"

"No. That's why Taylor wanted him out. I don't know for sure, but the way I heard it, your old man was about to blow the whole thing open. He'd found out what Taylor and the others were doing, and he was about to grass them up."

"So what happened?" I asked.

"He never got the chance to grass them up. He wanted to make sure he had enough evidence to back up what he said. He was still looking into things when he got killed." Marcus looked at me. "The drug raid was a set-up. Taylor knew what your dad was doing, so he set up the raid, made sure your dad was alone, and blackmailed some low-life to whack him."

"Shit," I whispered.

"Yeah, I know ... I'm sorry."

"Taylor killed my dad just to stop him talking?" I said.

"Well, Taylor didn't do it himself, not *personally*. I mean, he didn't pull the trigger. But yeah, he ordered the hit."

"What happened to the guy who *did* pull the trigger?"

"He died a few weeks later. From a suspected overdose," Marcus said.

"Suspected? What d'you mean?"

Marcus shrugged. "It was all covered up. No one could be sure."

"Shit," I said again.

I didn't know what else to say. It was just so ... I don't know. So wrong. So stupid. So pathetic.

I looked at Marcus. "Why?"

He frowned at me. "Why? I just told you why –"

"No, I mean why didn't you tell me this before? Why didn't Mum tell me? Why didn't *anyone* tell me?"

For the next half-hour, Marcus tried to explain why no one had told me. There were lots of reasons and it was all very complicated. But, in the end, it all came down to whispers and rumours.

The rumours had started after Dad died – rumours that *he* was corrupt, that *he* was the one who'd been stealing drugs and selling them on. There were other rumours, too – all kinds of nasty stuff. But Dad was dead now, and he'd died a hero, so everyone kept their mouths shut. And, even more important, he'd been a policeman. The police didn't want to talk about one of their men.

"Who started these rumours?" I asked Marcus.

"Who do you think?"

Jack Taylor.

And, Marcus explained, Taylor just happened to be a very good friend of Dad's wife, Sonia Cherry. He knew about Dad's affair with my mum. He knew that they'd had a child together – yours truly. That was another reason for everyone to keep their mouths shut. There was a grieving widow to consider.

"Not that she grieved all that much," Marcus added.

"How do you know?" I asked him.

He shrugged. "People talk ... you hear things ..."

"Do you know her? Dad's wife. I mean, do you know what she's like?"

"Not really. All I know is, she seemed to get over your dad's death pretty quick, and she lives in a nice big house."

"Has she got any kids?"

"I don't know."

"What about my mum?" I asked Marcus. "Does she know about any of this?"

He looked away. "You'll have to ask her about that."

I could tell he knew more than he was letting on, but I guessed he was right – it wasn't his job to tell me what my mum knew. That was between her and me. The only thing was, I didn't know how to ask her about it. I *wanted* to talk to her about Dad. I *wanted* to ask her questions and find out how much she knew. But I couldn't. Something was stopping me. I didn't know what it was.

Was I scared of the truth?

Was I scared of finding out that she'd hidden things from me?

Was I scared she wouldn't tell me anything?

Or was I scared of upsetting her? Scared of reminding her of the past?

My mum and her mum came to England from a little farming village in the north of Mexico when my mum was a baby.

She never knew who her father was.

Her mother died soon after they'd arrived in England, and Mum never found out why they'd had to leave Mexico. But the rest of her family wouldn't take her back, and Mum had to stay here. She lived in kids' homes or with foster parents until she was old enough to take care of herself.

She's had a hard life.

Why should I make it any worse?

I looked at Marcus. He'd stood up now and was buttoning his coat.

"Are you going?" I asked him.

He nodded. "Lots to do. Business is tricky with all this gang stuff going on. It's hard to make a living when the estate is crawling with cops all the time."

I watched him as he put on his hat and his gloves. I didn't know where he was going or what he was going to do when he got there.

I don't know how Marcus makes his living. I don't think anyone knows, apart from him. All I know is that he makes deals. He doesn't deal drugs, but he buys and sells just about everything else, and that includes information. And he knows everything there is to know about the estate.

"This guy who shot my dad," I said to him, "the low-life that Taylor blackmailed into killing him – what was his name?"

"He's dead," Marcus said. "I already told you that."

"I know."

"So why do you want to know his name?"

"Did he live on the estate?"

"Yeah ... in the East Tower."

"Did he have any family?"

"There's a sister –"

"I want to talk to her."

"She won't tell you anything."

"Why not?"

"She's scared of Taylor. She knows what he did to her brother, and she knows what he'll do to her if she doesn't keep her mouth shut. And even if she did start talking, she's so out of it on drugs all the time that no one would believe anything she said. She's a total mess, Johnny. And Taylor keeps her well supplied, so she *stays* a total mess."

"What's her name?"

"I really don't think this is a good idea –"

"What's her *name*, Marcus?"

He sighed again. "You're not going to leave this alone, are you?"

"No."

"You're going after Taylor, aren't you?"

"Yeah."

"He's not with the police any more."

"I know."

Marcus looked at me. "You've already been checking him out?"

"Not really. I just looked him up on the internet. *Jack Taylor Associates – Commercial and Private Investigations.*" I smiled at Marcus. "He's a private detective."

"And now you're going to investigate him?"

"Yeah."

Marcus sniffed, wiped his nose. "And what if I told you to leave it alone? What if I told you to forget all about it, that all you're going to do is get yourself killed? Would you listen to me?"

"No."

"You never learn, do you?" he said.

"What do you mean?"

"This private detective stuff ... I mean, I know that's what you want to be, but look what happened last time you started snooping around. You got beaten up. You got drugged. You almost got Della thrown off the roof."

"This is different –"

"No, it's not."

I looked at him. "All right," I said, "what would you do if you were me? What would you do if *you* found out that *your* dad was murdered, and that the guy who set up the hit was still out there? Would *you* leave it alone? Would *you* just forget it?"

As soon as I'd said it, I knew it was a stupid thing to say. Because Marcus's dad had been murdered. He'd been killed in prison just after Della was born. Someone had stabbed him in the neck with a sharpened spoon. And now I could see Marcus thinking about it, remembering it. I wished I'd kept my mouth shut.

"Sorry, Marcus," I started to say, "I didn't mean –"

"Robbie Franks," he said.

"What?"

"The guy Taylor hired to shoot your old man – his name was Robbie Franks. His sister's called Tisha." Marcus started to walk away. "Meet me outside the North Tower at ten o'clock tomorrow morning and I'll take you to see her."

After Marcus left, I stayed in the shed for another hour or so, not doing anything. I just stared at the floor, thinking about things. Me, my dad, Marcus, Della, Robbie Franks, Tisha Franks ... what I felt about everything ... the past, the present, the future ... what I wanted to do, what I was going to do.

I thought about it.

I tried to work it all out.

Then I gave up thinking and went home.

CHAPTER 3
TISHA FRANKS

When Marcus showed up at ten the next morning, I saw big Benny Toogood coming along behind him. I was pleased to see him.

"All right?" Marcus said to me.

I nodded at him, then smiled at Toog. He looked as big as ever – big, slow and silent. Toog never says very much. But then, when you're that big, you don't *need* to say very much. He was wearing a suit today – don't ask me why. No coat, just a second-hand suit that was about three sizes too small for him. He was also wearing a bright red bobble hat and wellington boots.

"Looking good, Toog," I told him.

He nodded at me.

I turned to Marcus. "Are we expecting trouble?" I thought maybe that's why Toog had come along.

"Not really," Marcus said. "I just thought Toog might like to join us for a while, that's all." He smiled at me. "You ready?"

"Yeah."

"Let's go, then."

As we headed across the square towards the East Tower, it began to get dark and a miserable grey sleet started to fall.

Tisha Franks's flat was on the seventh floor. Her mother let us in. She was a cold-eyed black woman, about 45 years old. She was wearing a thick woolly coat, a black beret, and a pair of fluffy bunny slippers on her feet. Her face was a sickly grey colour. She didn't look at any of us, and she never said a single word. She just opened the front door, showed us into the front room, then turned round and left.

Tisha was slumped on a grubby settee in the middle of the room. She was really skinny, you could see her bones, and her face was empty and hollow. Her clothes were supposed to be skin-tight but they hung loosely on her body. It was hard to tell her age. Tisha had the face and body of a young girl, but her eyes looked old and tired. I guessed she was in her mid-twenties. She was staring blankly at a wide-screen TV when we came in, and she didn't seem to notice we were there.

But the two guys sitting either side of her did.

The one on her left was a big black guy with a shaved head and gold chains round his neck. The other one was a skinny little mixed-race kid. He looked about the same age as me, fifteen or sixteen.

"All right, Danny?" Marcus said to the kid.

The kid said nothing.

Marcus nodded at the big guy and said to Danny, "What's he doing here?"

Danny said nothing and stared at Marcus. He was trying to look tough, but he didn't really have the face for it. Marcus smiled at him, then turned to me. "Danny is Tisha's step-brother," he told me. "He's from the West Tower, but he's been running with the E Boys for the last couple of months. He thinks it's a smart move." Marcus shook his head. "It's a pity, really ... if he wasn't so dumb he'd be a pretty good kid." Marcus looked over at the big guy. "This one calls himself Streak," he told me. "Danny thinks he's looking after Tish, but my guess is he's been told to keep an eye on Danny." Marcus grinned at the big guy. "Isn't that right, Streak?"

Streak just glared at him.

"You can go," Marcus told him.

"I ain't going nowhere," Streak said.

"I'm not asking you, I'm telling you."

"I ain't going –"

"Last chance," Marcus told him. "You can either leave by the door or you can leave by the window. It's up to you."

Streak looked up at Toog, who was standing there staring down at him. Streak was big, but compared to Toog he was nothing. Toog is huge – huge head, huge hands, huge shoulders. I could see Streak thinking about it, weighing up his chances, wondering if Toog would really throw him out of the window. It didn't take him long to make up his mind.

"Yeah, all right," he muttered, getting to his feet. "I was going anyway."

"Of course you were," Marcus said.

Streak looked at Danny as he walked towards the door. "I'll see you later," he said to him.

It sounded like a threat, but Danny said nothing.

Marcus waited until Streak had left the room, then he nodded at Toog to close the door, and he sat down on the settee next to Tisha. "Hey, Tish," he said to her, "it's me, Marcus. Marcus Hood. You remember me, don't you?"

Tisha rolled her eyes and looked at him. She seemed half-asleep. "Whuh?" she muttered.

Marcus looked into her eyes. "Listen, Tish, I need to talk to you about something. Is that all right? I just want to ask you a few questions –"

"Hold on," Danny cut in. "I'm not sure about this. What if Tisha doesn't want to talk to you?"

Marcus looked at him. "Shut up, Danny. I'm talking to Tisha – OK? If she doesn't want to talk to me, she can tell me herself. All right?"

"Yeah, but –"

"All *right*?"

Danny nodded.

Marcus stared at him for a moment, then turned back to Tisha. "It's about Robbie," he said to her. "I know it's a long time ago, but it's really important ..." She was staring at the TV again. Marcus clicked his fingers in front of her eyes to get her attention. "Tish?" he said. "Hey, Tisha?"

She looked at him. "Uh?"

"Tell us about your brother. Can you remember what happened to him?"

"Robbie's dead," she said sleepily.

"Yeah, I know –"

"He didn't wanna do it ..."

"Do what?" Marcus said. "He didn't want to do what?"

Tisha shook her head. "Can't say ..." She looked over at me, trying to focus her eyes. "Who's that?"

"That's Johnny," Marcus told her. "His dad used to work for Jack Taylor. You know Jack Taylor, don't you?"

Her eyes went cold. "Yeah ... dirty bastard." She gave Danny a quick look, then she leaned forward and whispered to Marcus, "He killed Robbie."

"Jack Taylor killed Robbie?"

"Uh-huh."

"How?"

"Give him some bad shit ..." she said with a dopey grin. "Good stuff ... nearly pure ... scrambled his brains."

"Why did he do that?"

"Who ... Robbie?"

"No, why did Taylor kill Robbie?"

She grinned again, this time tapping a finger to the side of her nose. "Secret," she muttered. "It's a secret ..."

Marcus sighed. "Listen to me, Tisha ... listen. It's not a secret. Everyone knows what Robbie did."

Tisha shook her head. "He didn't wanna do it … Taylor made him. He was gonna send Robbie down if he didn't do it …"

"I know," Marcus said. "The thing is, Tisha, the guy that Robbie killed …" He looked at me, then turned back to Tisha. "It was Johnny's dad."

"Who's Johnny?"

"Me," I said. "I'm Johnny."

She looked up at me. "Uh?"

"Your brother killed my dad."

"He didn't wanna …"

"Yeah, I know. Jack Taylor made him do it. Then Taylor killed Robbie. And now he's killing you."

She blinked sadly at me.

"Don't you care?" I said to her.

She didn't say anything, she just kept on staring at me. I could see Marcus looking at me too, and I knew he wanted me to shut up and leave the talking to him, but I just couldn't stop myself.

"Doesn't it bother you?" I said to Tisha. "Your brother's dead, and you know who killed him, and all you're doing is lying around here all day, whacked out of your head –"

"You don't know what it's like," she said, angry now. "You don't know *shit*."

"Don't you want Taylor to pay for Robbie's death?"

"What's the point? It won't make no difference, will it? Robbie ain't coming back whatever I do." She shook her head, trying to clear her mind. "What can I do, anyway? I only gotta fart and Taylor knows about it. I can't do nothing."

"What about me?"

"What *about* you?"

"I'm not scared of Taylor. If I can prove what he did, I'll get him put away for the rest of his life."

"You think so?"

"Yeah."

She laughed. "He'll stomp the shit out of you."

"At least I'm willing to try."

"That's cos you're stupid."

I looked at her. She was angry. Her voice sounded nasty but her eyes were brimming with tears. I looked at Marcus. He shrugged, as if to say – I *told* you this was a waste of time. I looked back at Tisha again. Danny was holding her hand now. She was sitting perfectly still. She didn't make a sound as the tears streamed down her face. It was like watching a dead girl weep.

Danny looked at me. There was hatred in his eyes, hatred and sadness.

"I'm sorry," I told him. "I didn't mean ... I didn't know ... I'm sorry. We'll go now." I turned to Marcus. "Come on, let's get out of here."

Marcus got to his feet and nodded at Toog, and we all started heading for the door.

"Wait a minute," Tisha called out. "Hold on ..."

I turned round and saw her trying to get up from the settee. She seemed so weak she couldn't have got up if Danny hadn't helped her.

"I'm all right," she said to Danny. "I'm all right."

He let go of her, and she began walking slowly across the room. She stopped in front of a cupboard, held onto it for a moment, then crouched down in front of it and opened a drawer. She started to hunt around inside for something. I glanced at Marcus.

"What's she doing?" I whispered.

He shrugged.

I looked back at Tisha. She'd stood up again and was coming over to us. She stopped in front of me like she was thinking about it, then passed me a piece of paper. I looked at it. It was a page torn from a notebook – tattered and creased, folded in half.

"Take it," Tisha said to me. "Robbie left it for me. It was in a sealed envelope. Maybe it's no good for nothing, but it's all I got." She gave me a sad smile. "And you didn't get it from me – all right?"

I nodded at her, not sure what to say.

She stood there looking at me for a while, then she turned round and went back over to the settee. Danny took her by the hand and gently helped her to sit back down. I wanted to say goodbye to her, but she was gone again now. She'd slumped back onto the settee and her eyes were fixed blankly on the TV screen.

Danny didn't look at us as we left the room.

In the lift on the way back down, I unfolded the tattered bit of paper she'd given me and read what was written on it. It was a note from Robbie to Tisha, written in pencil. The handwriting was scrawled as if he'd scribbled it in a hurry. It said –

Tish, I hope you're not reading this cos if you are it means I'm dead. But you know I got mixed up in some bad stuff and you know I didn't want do it but there was nothing I could do about it. Anyway, if anything happens to me, it's Taylor, OK? He made me hit that cop and now he's going to take me out.

Just so you know. I love you.

Robbie.

CHAPTER 4
JACK TAYLOR

Later that afternoon, I caught a bus to the tube station and took a train into town. I got off at Paddington, checked the map on my phone, then started walking. The sleet was turning to snow now, and the sky was so dark that it felt like the middle of the night.

It didn't take long to get where I was going, and ten minutes later I was standing outside a small office block in a quiet street just off Baker Street. The windows were tinted, so I couldn't see inside, but I knew this was the right place. Across the window were gold letters that said – **Jack Taylor Associates – Commercial and Private Investigations**.

I took a deep breath, opened the door and went inside.

It was an expensive-looking place – thick carpets, leather chairs, magazines on a low glass table. There was a smart coffee machine and fancy paintings on the wall. At the far end of the waiting area there were two closed doors. In front of the doors, set against the wall, was the reception desk. A young blonde woman was sitting behind the desk. Sleek clothes, slick hair, a stunning face. She was one of those women who are so good-looking they make you feel stupid.

As I came in and walked over to the reception desk, she didn't even glance at me. She just sat there, looking cool and staring at something on a computer screen. I stopped in front of the desk. She still didn't look at me. I coughed to get her attention. She ignored me for another second or two. Then she tapped her keyboard – once, twice – and looked up at me at last.

"Yes?" she said.

I smiled at her. "I'd like to see Mr Taylor, please."

"Do you have an appointment?"

"No. I just thought –"

"Mr Taylor is a very busy man," she said. "If you want to see him, you'll have to make an appointment." She gave me a quick, cold smile, then turned back to the computer screen and started tapping away at the keyboard.

"Is he busy now?" I asked her.

"Yes," she said, without looking up.

"It won't take long ... I only want to see him for a minute."

She stopped typing and looked up at me. "As I said, you'll have to make an appointment. Now, if you'll excuse me, I have work to do."

She went back to her typing.

I just stood there, watching her. I knew she could still see me, but she wasn't going to look at me. So I just waited. After a while she gave a sigh, stopped typing, and looked at me again.

I smiled at her. "I'm still here."

"So I see."

"Couldn't you just let Mr Taylor know I'm here? I don't mind waiting."

She shook her head. "If you don't go now, I'm afraid I'll have to ask someone to show you out."

"Five minutes," I said. "That's all I want ..."

"Right," she said. "That's it. I'm calling Security." She started to reach for the phone, but just as she was about to hit a button, one of the doors behind her opened and three people came out – a man, a woman and a girl. The man was tall and heavy, with very short silvery-grey hair. He had his arm around the woman's shoulder and they were smiling at each other as if they'd just shared a secret.

The girl was about 16 or 17 years old, and she had to be the woman's daughter. They had the same elegant face, the same dark eyes, the same proud look. They were even wearing the same designer clothes – designer-smart for the mother, designer-scruffy for the daughter. But there was something about the girl that made her different from her mother ... something that made me feel odd, as if I knew her. I didn't know what it was, but somehow it made me remember something ... or someone ...

I looked at the receptionist. She still had her finger ready to press the security button on the phone, but now she was looking over at the grey-haired man. As he kissed the woman and the girl goodbye and watched them walk out, his smile vanished and he glanced over at me. When he saw me, his face seemed to darken for a moment. Then, almost at once, he smiled again and looked over at the receptionist.

"Everything all right, Mandy?" he asked.

"I was ... uhh ... I was just calling Security, Mr Taylor," she told him.

"Really?" He glanced at me again, then back at Mandy. "Is something wrong?"

"This gentleman refuses to leave," she said. "I told him you were busy, but he won't listen to me."

"Is that right?" He smiled at me. "What's your problem, son?"

"Nothing, I just wanted to see you for a minute, that's all."

"About what?"

I pretended to be embarrassed. "It's just ... well, it's just that I've always wanted to be a private detective, you know ... like you. And I was hoping you could give me some advice. I've read about you, you know ... I've read about some of your cases ..."

"Really?"

"Yeah ..."

He smiled again, then looked over at the receptionist. "What time's my next meeting, Mandy?"

"Three o'clock," she told him. "Barton Insurance."

He glanced at his watch, then started to go back into his office. "Come on, then," he said to me. "I can give you 15 minutes."

His office was warm and comfortable. There was a big oak desk, shelves full of books, more leather chairs. The walls were covered with framed certificates and photos. Most of the pictures showed Jack Taylor posing with famous faces – TV celebrities, footballers, people I'd seen on the news – but one or two of them had been taken when he was a policeman.

There was a young Jack Taylor in his uniform, Jack Taylor at a press conference, Jack Taylor arresting a famous criminal. There was even one of Jack Taylor at a police funeral. There he was, with loads of other policemen, all of them dressed up in their uniforms and medals. Somehow I just knew it was my dad's funeral. Standing beside Jack Taylor in the photo was a woman in black, dabbing at her eyes with a handkerchief. I couldn't be sure, but she looked like the woman I'd seen coming out of his office a few minutes ago.

I looked at Taylor now as he sat at his desk – cold and hard and confident. Did he have any idea who I was?

"Sit down, son," he told me, and he waved at a chair. "What's your name?"

"Vernon," I said, as I sat down opposite him. "Vernon Small."

He smiled at me. "So, Vernon … you want to be a private detective, do you?"

He spent the next ten minutes telling me all about himself and his company. "I did this, *blah blah blah* … my company does that, *blah blah blah* … I know everything, *blah blah blah* …"

I just sat there and nodded and smiled as he droned on and on. I wasn't really listening to him.

I couldn't listen to him. As I stared into his cold grey eyes, the only voice I could hear was the voice of hate inside my head.

'You killed my dad,' it was saying.

You killed my dad.

You killed my dad.

YOU KILLED MY DAD ...

"It's not true," I heard Taylor say.

"What?" I said, suddenly alert. "What isn't true?"

He frowned at me. "I just *told* you – the way private detectives behave in films and on TV ... it's just not true. We don't carry guns or get into fights. We don't chase around all over the place in fast cars. That's all make-believe. We spend most of our time talking on the phone or sitting in front of a computer." He shook his head. "You need proper skills to be a private detective. It's a business, just like any other business. The best advice I can give you is to get a good education. Take your A-levels, go to university, then join the police or the armed forces. Get yourself some experience. Then, once you've done all that, come back and see me." He grinned. "You never know, I might even give you a job."

"If you're still around then," I said.

He smiled coldly at me. "I'll still be around, son. Don't you worry about that."

I glanced at the pictures of him on the wall. "Did you like being a policeman?" I asked him.

He nodded. "Best years of my life."

"So why did you leave?"

He stared at me. For a moment, I could see he was angry. Then he smiled again.

"I needed a new challenge," he said. "It was time to move on, simple as that." He looked at his watch. "And now I'm afraid it's time for you to move on." He got to his feet. "Well, Vernon, I'm sorry we couldn't talk for very long, but I hope I've given you something to think about."

"Yeah, plenty, thanks. You've been really helpful. Can I just ask you one more thing?"

He glanced at his watch again. "What is it?"

"Well, I was just thinking about something ..."

I looked right into his eyes.

"If you're trying to make a case against someone ... if you're trying to prove that they've done something wrong ... what's the best way to do it?"

Taylor stared at me for a long time then – his eyes cold, his face empty and blank. After what seemed like hours, his face broke into a smile again, and he moved out from behind his desk and started walking over to the door.

"Evidence," he told me, "that's what you need. You need the evidence to prove someone's done something. Without evidence, there's no proof. And if you don't have any proof, you might as well give up." He opened the door and waited for me. "I'd remember that if I were you, Vernon. No evidence, no proof." He winked at me. "Bear it in mind."

The receptionist, Mandy, didn't look at me on the way out. She was too busy tapping away at her keyboard again. I walked past her desk, then stopped and turned round, as if I'd suddenly remembered something.

"Keys," I said.

Mandy looked up. "Excuse me?"

"Mr Taylor said to ask you if they'd left their keys."

"Who?"

I scratched my head. "Sorry ... I've forgotten their names ... the woman and the girl he was with just now ..."

"You mean Mrs Cherry and Pippa?"

"Yeah, that's it. Did they leave their keys with you?"

"What keys? Why would they leave their keys with me?"

I shrugged. "I don't know ... Mr Taylor just asked me to ask you."

She looked at me and shook her head, as if I was an idiot.

"Oh, well," I said, "not to worry." I flashed a smile at her. "It was nice meeting you, Mandy. Thanks for all your help. I'll see you later."

I might have looked and sounded OK as I walked out of the office, but I wasn't. My head was reeling. I could barely think straight. The woman I'd seen with Taylor was Mrs Cherry ... Sonia Cherry ... my dad's wife ... the woman in black in the funeral photo ... my dad's widow. And the girl ... the daughter ... Pippa. If she was Sonia's daughter, if she really *was* Sonia's daughter ...

Did that mean she was my dad's daughter too?

My dad's daughter ...

My sister ...

My big sister ...

'God,' I thought to myself, 'have I got a sister?'

Is that why I thought I'd seen her before?

I still felt odd and confused as I left the building and started heading back to the tube station. I wasn't looking at the car that pulled up outside Taylor's office. But then something made me glance back, and I saw two men getting out of the car. One of them had a hood up, so I couldn't see his face. But I knew who the other one was. He was a big guy – shaved head, gold chains round his neck.

It was Streak.

I saw him say something to the hooded guy, then the hooded guy slapped Streak on the shoulder, and they both went into Taylor's office.

CHAPTER 5
SNOW AND FIRE

I had a lot to think about now, and most of it didn't make sense. What was Sonia Cherry doing with Taylor? What was Streak doing at Taylor's office? And why had no one ever told me I had a sister?

Did Mum know?

Did Marcus know?

And what did I think about it?

I didn't know.

I didn't really know anything.

All I'd been doing was trying to stir things up, trying to make something happen. But I didn't know what good it would do. And now that I *had* made something happen, I still didn't know what good it would do.

Had I got any real evidence that Taylor had ordered Robbie Franks to kill my dad?

No.

Had I got any real evidence that Taylor had killed Robbie Franks?

No.

Had I got any evidence of anything?

No.

No evidence, no proof.

All I'd got was a head full of questions.

It was about 9 p.m. when I got back to the estate. The night was cold and black, the snow was still falling, and there were loads of police cars parked over the road. As I headed across the square towards the North Tower, I could see two or three burning cars over by the East Tower. Another fire was starting to burn in a skip outside the West Tower. Thick black smoke hung in the air. The orange lights of the flickering flames and the flashing blue lights of the police cars shimmered in the fresh white snow.

There were E Boys and Westies everywhere – hanging around outside the tower blocks, watching from the windows, waiting in the shadows. Most of them wore hoodies and caps, or scarves pulled up to hide their faces. Some of them were even wearing Santa hats.

It was like a Christmas nightmare.

Most times the North Tower stays out of it when there's gang stuff going on. But that night, as I went into the lobby and headed over to the lifts, there were crowds of people all over the place. A lot of them were just people who lived there. They'd come down to find out what was going on. But I also saw a few E Boys and Westies, most of them young kids, trying to drum up support for their gangs.

As I pushed my way through the crowds towards the lift, I heard a voice calling out. "Hey, Johnny D, hold on ... hey!"

I looked round and saw Toog. He was like a bulldozer pushing through the crowd towards me. Marcus was following him. They came up to me, and Toog stood aside to let Marcus through.

"Where've you been?" he asked me. "Your mum's been looking for you."

"Why?" I said.

"Why do you think? The shit's going down, that's why. She was worried about you."

"Why didn't she ring me?" I asked.

"The cops have had the local mobile networks closed down so the gangs can't use their phones."

"Is Mum all right?"

"Yeah, she's fine ..." Marcus said.

"What about your mum and Della?" I wanted to know.

"They're OK."

I saw Marcus glance through the doors, and then I saw what he was looking at. A large group of Westies were moving out of the West Tower into the square. Across the road, a fire engine had arrived, and policemen in riot gear were spilling out of the backs of patrol vans.

Marcus looked at me. "We need to get up to our floor before it all starts kicking off down here."

"Let's go, then," I said.

I started heading off towards the lift, but Marcus grabbed me and pulled me back.

"Forget the lift," he said, "there's too many people. We'll have to use the stairs."

Walking up 17 flights of stairs takes a long time. It takes even longer when you have to keep fighting your way past gangs of idiots who are trying to stop you from going up. They didn't have any reason to stop us, they were just looking for trouble – any kind of trouble – and there were only three of us, so they thought we were easy meat. But they hadn't reckoned on Toog. And that was a big mistake. A lot of people got their heads cracked on the stairs that night.

Getting upstairs took time. When we got to the 17th floor at last, it looked like we might be too late. The lift doors at the end of the hallway were jammed open and there were Westies running around everywhere – kicking in doors, shouting and screaming, ransacking flats. As Toog marched down the hallway and started wading into them, Marcus ran over to his flat and jumped through the smashed-in doorway.

"Mum!" he called out, "Della! Where are you? Are you all right? Mum!!"

The door to my flat suddenly opened and Mum popped her head out. "Johnny!" she cried out. "Get in here."

I looked down the hallway and saw Toog smashing heads against the wall and Westies running for the lift. Then Marcus came flying out of his flat, dragging an Eminem lookalike by the neck. "Where are they?" Marcus hissed at him.

"I dunno –" the guy muttered.

Marcus punched him in the face.

"*Where are they?*"

"Marcus!" Mum yelled at him. "Your mum and Della are in here with me."

Marcus looked at her.

"They're safe, Marcus," Mum said. "Let him go."

Marcus nodded at her and let the kid go. He ran off down the hallway, blood dripping from his face. I watched him swerve round Toog and jump into the lift with the rest of the Westies. There were six or seven of them – not as many as I'd thought when we first got up there. Toog had given them a good hammering. Those that weren't lying on the floor were bleeding, or limping, or both. The biggest one, a kid of about 18 with a busted nose, gave Toog the finger. Then he quickly hit the lift button as Toog started towards him. As the lift doors closed, I heard the kid shout out, "We'll be back! You hear me? We gonna burn you out tonight!"

CHAPTER 6

THE NIGHT GOES ON

It wasn't safe to stay in a flat with no door, so Marcus and Della and their mum spent the rest of the night with me and Mum in our flat. Toog stayed with us, too. Marcus fixed the lift so it wouldn't stop at the 17th floor and Toog dragged a heavy wardrobe from Marcus's flat and jammed it up against the stairwell door. That way no one could get on to our landing. Once he'd done that, and everyone was back in our flat, we made a big heap of chairs and a table against the front door. Then we settled down to wait out the night.

It was good to see Della again ... it was kind of odd, too. Her mum kept watching us, making sure we didn't get too close. We had to wait until her mum went into the kitchen before we could say hello to each other properly. And even then, Marcus and Toog were standing over at the window, watching the riot down below, so it was still a bit awkward.

But I didn't really care.

I went over and sat down next to her on the settee.

"Are you all right?" I asked her.

She smiled at me. "I am now."

I glanced over at Marcus. He grinned and blew a kiss at me.

"Just ignore him," Della said.

I turned back to her. "What happened earlier? When those guys broke into your flat ... I mean, they didn't hurt you or anything, did they?"

She shook her head. "They just told us to get out ... then they started ransacking the place. I don't think they meant any harm. They were just looking for stuff to nick." She smiled at me again. I just stared at her. She looked wonderful – glistening curls of short blonde hair, eyes like jewels, sparkling white teeth. She looked so good, it hurt.

"You've had your brace taken off," I said.

She put her hand up behind her head and pouted her lips like a supermodel. "I had it done this morning," she said. "What do you think?"

"Very nice."

"Really?" She closed her mouth and ran a finger over her lips. "It still feels a bit odd, but at least my mouth doesn't taste of metal any more." She smiled shyly and leaned towards me. "Do you want to see how it tastes?"

Just then Della's mum came back into the room. She was carrying a big plate of sandwiches. When she saw Della sitting so close to me, she gave me a dirty look.

"What's going on?" she said sharply.

"Nothing," I muttered. I moved away from Della. "We were just ... you know ... we were just talking."

"It didn't *look* like talking."

"Oh, come *on*, Mum," Della said. "If we're all going to be stuck here for the rest of the night, we might as well try to get on with each other. Just give Johnny a chance ... he's not as bad as you think."

"No?"

Della grinned at me. "You're a good boy, aren't you, Johnny?"

God, I was embarrassed.

"All right," Mrs Hood said slowly, "I'll give him a chance ... but just for tonight. After that ... well, we'll see how it goes." She glared at me. "And don't think I won't be watching you, because I will. Do you understand?"

I nodded at her.

My mum came into the room then. I didn't know if she'd heard what Mrs Hood had just said, but I saw her wink at me, so I guessed she had.

"Right, then," she said. "Who wants coffee and who wants tea?"

The night went on.

Mum talked to Mrs Hood and I talked softly to Della, and Marcus and Toog stayed over at the window, watching the estate go up in flames. Every half-hour or so, I went over and watched too. Every time I looked out of the window, things were getting worse. Cars were burning everywhere. Hundreds of policemen in riot gear were trying to keep the E Boys and the Westies apart, and both gangs were fighting the police. There were bricks flying all over the place, little kids throwing stones, and petrol bombs coming out of the tower block windows. There were ambulances, fire engines, and then reporters and TV crews came to join in. It was a mess.

"How long do you think it's going to last?" I asked Marcus.

He shrugged. "It won't stop until one of the gangs has taken control. It could be hours, it could be days. All we can do is wait."

I looked down at the square as another petrol bomb came flying out of the West Tower and exploded in a ball of flame. Thick clouds of black smoke puffed up into the burning night sky. The snow kept falling.

"Can I talk to you for a minute?" I said to Marcus. "In private."

We went into my bedroom and shut the door and I told Marcus about going to see Taylor. When I'd finished telling him everything, he didn't say anything. For a long time he just sat there thinking.

In the silence of my bedroom, I could hear the faint sounds of the riot going on down below. It seemed like a long way away.

"Why did you go to see Taylor?" Marcus said at last.

"I don't know ... I just wanted to see him, I suppose. See what he looked like."

Marcus nodded. "And you're sure you don't know who the other guy was – the one you saw going into Taylor's office with Streak?"

"No, he had his hood up. What do you think Streak was doing there?"

"I think he was telling Taylor about our visit to Tisha Franks," Marcus said. "Taylor still controls a lot of the estate. He works with the E Boys and the

Westies, and he's got most of the local cops in his pocket too. The investigation business is mostly just a front. He makes his money from drugs, just like he always did."

"You could have told me this before," I said.

"I tried to, but you wouldn't listen."

"Why didn't you tell me about Taylor and Sonia Cherry?"

"I told you they were friends –"

"Yeah, but they're more than just *friends*, aren't they?"

Marcus shrugged.

"Come *on*," I said to him. "I know you know something."

He sighed. "I don't *know* anything ... I've just heard rumours."

"What rumours?"

He thought for a moment, then said, "Jack Taylor's been seeing Sonia Cherry for years. They were having an affair when your dad was still alive. Taylor used to keep Sonia company when your dad was seeing your mum."

"Did she know?" I asked.

"Who?"

"Sonia. Did she know that her husband was having an affair with my mum?"

"I don't know ... I suppose so," Marcus said.

"When did Taylor start seeing Sonia? I mean, could *he* be Pippa's dad?" I was starting to sound panicky.

"Who the hell's Pippa?" Marcus wanted to know.

"Did Sonia have anything to do with Dad's death?"

"For Christ's sake, Johnny," Marcus said angrily. "I don't *know* – OK?" He shook his head. "Look, I know how much this means to you, but I'm not going to tell you stuff unless I know for a fact that it's true. I mean, yeah, Taylor is probably still seeing Sonia Cherry and, yeah, maybe she had something to do with your dad's death. But I don't know that, do I? All I know is –"

He stopped talking as the bedroom door suddenly opened, and we both looked over to see Della standing in the doorway.

"Toog says you'd better come quick," she told us. "Jack Taylor's coming."

CHAPTER 7
GOING UP

I followed Marcus out of the bedroom and we hurried into the front room and joined Toog at the window. He pointed down at the square. It was a long way down, and it was hard to make anything out through all the smoke and the crowds and the burning fires, but I could see enough to know that Toog was right. A group of about twenty men was coming round the edge of the square, heading towards the North Tower, and right in the middle of the group was the grey-haired head of Jack Taylor. Some of his men were wearing hoodies and caps, and some of them had scarves over their faces, but they weren't all E Boys or Westies. Some of his men were even in riot gear, and one of them was carrying a black police-issue battering ram.

"What's Taylor doing here?" I asked Marcus.

"I don't know," Marcus said. "But my guess is he's coming after you." He looked at me. "You've been stirring things up too much, Johnny. Asking too many questions. Taylor's using the riot as cover."

"Cover for what?"

"For getting rid of you."

"What's going on?"

I turned round and saw Mum standing behind us.

"Who's getting rid of who?" she said to me.

I looked at Marcus.

"Tell her," he said.

"It's Jack Taylor," I said to Mum.

Her eyes widened. "Taylor?" she gasped. "What's he got to do with anything?"

"Well," I said, "it's a long story –"

"We haven't got time for stories right now," Marcus said. He looked at Mum. "Johnny's been looking into his dad's death, and he's getting closer than Jack Taylor likes. Taylor's bringing his mob up here." Marcus glanced down through the window. "They've just entered the tower."

Mum looked at me. "Christ, Johnny ... what have you *done*?"

"I was just trying to find out about Dad," I told her. "I wanted to know what happened to him."

"Why didn't you *ask* me?" she said.

"Why didn't you tell me?"

"Because ..." she said hesitantly, "because it's all mixed up. And I knew if I told you the truth, you'd start digging into things ... you'd want to put things right. But you can't put things right, Johnny. No one can." She shook her head. "You can't fight against men like Jack Taylor. They never lose. I tried telling your dad that, but he wouldn't listen. And look what happened to him. I didn't want anything to happen to you."

"It won't," I said.

"That's exactly what your dad said."

I looked at Marcus. "What's Taylor going to do?"

"He'll try the lift first," Marcus said. "When he works out he can't use it to get up here, he'll cut the power, leave some of his men on the ground floor, and bring the rest up the stairs. We can probably hold them off for a while, but they'll get through in the end."

"Then what?"

"Then we've had it – all of us. He's not going to leave any witnesses. Whatever he does, he'll make it look like a random attack. Or maybe he'll just burn us out and blame it on the Westies."

"So we can't stay here," I said.

"No."

"And it's no good calling the police."

“All the phone lines are out.”

“And if we go down the stairs we’re going to run right into Taylor and his men.”

“Yeah.”

“So that just leaves the roof.”

Marcus nodded. “It’s not much of a choice, but there’s nowhere else. And at least we won’t get burned alive on the roof.”

I looked at Mum. “What do *you* think?”

She smiled sadly at me. “I think we’re in a lot of trouble.” She looked over at Mrs Hood and Della. “I’m sorry,” she told them, “but I think Marcus is right. We have to get out of here before Jack Taylor arrives, and the roof is our only choice.” She turned back to Marcus. “I think we should go right now, don’t you?”

Marcus grinned at her. “It wouldn’t be a bad idea.”

“OK,” Mum said. “Let’s do it.”

I went out into the hallway with Marcus and Toog and we dragged the wardrobe away from the stairwell door. Marcus stepped through the door and leaned over to look down the stairs.

“I can hear them coming,” he whispered. “They’re only a few floors away.”

"Mum! Della!" I called out softly. "Come on, hurry up!"

Della and Mrs Hood came out of the flat and walked quickly over to the door, but there was still no sign of Mum.

"What's she doing?" I asked Della.

Della shook her head. "She said she had to get something."

"They're almost here!" Marcus cut in.

Mum came out of the flat then. She had her handbag under her arm. I waved her over to the door, and Marcus started hurrying them all up to the roof. I could hear the sound of Taylor and his men coming up the stairs now – loud footsteps, muffled shouts. Just for a moment I stopped to think. What was all this about? Why was this happening? How had I got us into this? And why? Then Marcus suddenly grabbed me and shoved me towards the stairs.

"Go!" he hissed at me.

"What about –?"

"Just *go!*"

As I started running up the stairs, I heard a voice calling out from below. "They're here! They're going up –"

Then I heard a heavy thump. I turned round, looked down and saw a big kid sprawled on the stairs. He was holding his head and groaning, and Toog was standing over him.

Another shout rang out from below. "They're going up to the roof!"

"Shit!" said Marcus.

Toog looked at him.

"Come *on*!" I hissed. "Let's go!"

Marcus nodded at Toog, and we all started running up the stairs. We were running hard and our footsteps were clattering on the cold stone steps. Even so, I could still hear the sound of Taylor's men down below. Doors were slamming, glass was breaking, ugly voices were shouting and yelling.

"Shit! They got Jermaine!" I heard someone say, and I knew they must have found the kid Toog thumped.

"Leave him!" someone else shouted.

"Dev!" another voice yelled.

"Yo!"

"You and your boys trash the flat! Don't burn it yet – OK? The rest of you go on up to the roof."

CHAPTER 8
YOU'RE ON YOUR OWN, JACK

Mum, Della and Mrs Hood were waiting for us at the top of the stairs on the 23rd floor.

"We have to hurry," I told them. "Taylor knows where we're going. Follow me."

I led them down the corridor to a door marked PRIVATE – NO ENTRY. In front of the door, I stooped down and pulled out a key from beneath a piece of loose floor. Then I unlocked the door and pushed everyone inside.

"What is this place?" Mum asked me. "And how come you've got a key?"

"I'll tell you later," I said.

The door led us through into the little boiler room. At the other side of the room was an archway through to some steps, and at the top of the steps was the door to the roof. The boiler room was packed full of stuff – cupboards and shelves, boxes of tools, wires and cables – but as I locked the door behind us, I said to Marcus, "Some of us could hide in here."

He looked around. "Yeah ... it might work." He turned to his mum. "Mum, you stay here with Della and Mrs D. Hide behind those cupboards. When Taylor and his men get through the door, they'll head straight for the roof. Once they've gone, you go back down the stairs and get help."

"What about you?" she asked him. "What are you going to do?"

Suddenly we heard loud shouts from the corridor outside. We could hear running feet, excited voices, hands banging against the walls. Marcus started to move Della and his mum towards the cupboards.

"I'm not staying behind," Della protested. "I don't want to hide –"

"Do you want to help us or not?" Marcus said to her.

She looked at me. "Yeah ... I want to help you."

I nodded at her, and she got in behind the cupboards with her mum. I looked over at my mum.

She smiled at me. "No chance. I'm coming with you."

I looked at Marcus. He looked at Mum.

BOOM! – a battering ram thudded against the door.

The door shook but didn't break.

Marcus threw an old blanket over the cupboards, so Della and his mum were hidden. Then we all hurried off through the archway and up the steps to the roof.

The night sky was silent and black, and the roof was covered with a drift of pure white snow. It was beautiful. As the four of us walked across it, our breath misting in the icy air, I was smiling. I looked at Mum, who was walking beside me. She was smiling, too.

"It's nice up here, isn't it?" she said.

I nodded. "I come up here sometimes when I want to be on my own ... you know, when I need to think about things. See that metal shed over there? That's my secret place. Well, it used to be, anyway."

Mum looked at me. "We all need our secret places, Johnny."

I didn't know what to say to that, so I didn't say anything.

We went over to the edge of the roof and looked down. The riot was still going on. The fires were still burning. The snow was still falling. We stood there and watched it.

After a while, Marcus looked round. "Here they come," he said.

We all turned round. The door to the roof had opened and a hooded head was looking out. It was a tough-looking kid. I'd seen him around the estate, but I didn't know who he was. He saw us, stared at us for a moment, then smiled coldly and spoke to someone behind him. After a second or two, he stepped through the door and came out onto the roof.

Then another guy came out.

And another one.

And another.

They just kept coming.

By the time Taylor himself came out and shut the door, there must have been about fifteen or sixteen of them lined up in front of him. I knew some of them. Streak was there, his gold chains glinting in the starlight. And I could see Danny, Tisha's step-brother. But the rest of them were just faces – gang faces, cop faces, faces in the snow.

Taylor moved to the front of his men and they stood in a semi-circle behind him. Before they had a chance to move towards us, the four of us started walking towards them. We walked in a line – me, Mum, Marcus, and Toog – our feet crunching softly in the fresh white snow. We stopped in the middle of the roof, about five metres away from Taylor.

Taylor smiled at us. "Well, well," he said, "look who we've got here." He grinned at me, glanced at Marcus and Toog, then turned his attention to Mum. "It's good to see you, Maria. You're looking well."

Mum just stared at him.

"I had a nice little chat with Johnny this afternoon," he said to her. "Did he tell you about it? No? I didn't think so." Taylor shook his head. "I expected more of you, Maria. You ought to know about keeping your mouth shut. Your mother was Mexican." He grinned at her. "I mean, Mexicans ... they grow up with this kind of stuff, don't they?"

"What kind of stuff?" Mum said.

He smiled at her. "Oh, come on, you know what I mean – corruption, drugs, murder. You know what I did, Maria. You know what I do. And you know there's nothing you can do about it. It's just the way it is. You know that, Maria. And you know that all you can do is keep your mouth shut and get on with your life." He glanced at me, then back at Mum. "You should have brought up your mongrel kid to keep his mouth shut, too."

"You killed my dad," I said to him. "You forced Robbie Franks to shoot him, and then you had Robbie killed to cover it up."

Taylor stared at me. "So?"

I looked round at the men behind him and asked the one with the battering ram, "Did you know that Taylor killed a policeman? You can check it out," I said. "His name was David Cherry. He was a Detective Sergeant with the Drug Squad when Taylor was in charge. And you ..." I looked at Danny. "What the hell are you doing here? This bastard killed your step-brother. He's killing your step-sister. What's the matter with you?" I looked round at the rest of the men and I suddenly felt sick of it all. "What's the matter with all of you? Why are you so scared of this grey-haired piece of shit? Can't you see he's just using you ... that's what he does. He uses people. Uses them up, spits them out –"

"All right, kid," Taylor said softly, "that's enough."

"I can prove you killed Robbie Franks," I told him, and put my hand into my pocket. I pulled out the letter that Tisha had given me and waved it at Taylor. "See? I've got the evidence, just like you told me."

"You think that piece of crap is evidence?" Taylor sneered. "I don't think so." He pulled a pistol from his pocket. “Not that it matters anyway.” He passed the pistol to Danny. “Shoot him and get the letter.”

Danny didn’t move. “What?” he said.

“Here, take the gun.”

Danny shook his head. “I ain’t shooting no one.”

“Why not, for Christ’s sake? There’s a riot going on. No one’s going to know anything.”

Danny backed away from him. “Nah,” he muttered and shook his head, “this ain’t right ...”

Taylor glared at him for a moment, then he turned quickly and aimed the gun at me. “Give me the letter.”

“No.”

Taylor aimed the pistol at Mum and fired off a shot. The bullet thwacked into the ground an inch from her feet.

“Last chance, kid,” Taylor said, turning back to me. “The next one goes in her head. Now, give me the letter.”

I screwed up Tisha’s letter and dropped it on the ground.

Taylor glared at me for a moment, then he turned to Streak. “Get it,” he told him.

Streak came over, picked up the ball of paper, then went back and gave it to Taylor. Taylor didn't even bother looking at it, he just ripped the paper up, and threw the pieces into the air. "No evidence, no proof," he said to me.

He held out the pistol to Danny. "Clean it and get rid of it," he told him. "And if you ever say no to me again, I'll make sure Tisha gets the same shit as Robbie. You got that?"

Danny's eyes were full of hate as he took the gun from Taylor's hand, but he didn't say anything. He just put the pistol in his pocket and slowly backed away.

It was then that I felt something move beside me. I heard an angry sigh, and when I turned and looked at Mum, I couldn't believe what I was seeing. She was pulling a small pistol from her bag. Her eyes were dead and empty as she raised the gun and pointed it at Taylor. And when she spoke, her voice was as cold as ice.

"I should have done this years ago," she said.

Taylor stared at her for a second, then laughed. "What do you think you're doing?"

"What does it look like?"

"If you shoot me, you're dead," Taylor said.

"So are you," she told him.

Without taking his eyes off Mum, Taylor slowly held out his hand to Danny. "Give me the gun, boy," he said to him.

Danny backed further away.

Taylor gritted his teeth. "Give ... me ... the ... *gun*."

As Danny kept moving away from him, some of the others began edging backwards too. One step back, then another, and another ... and then suddenly they were all backing away from Taylor.

"Hey," he said, glancing over his shoulder, "what the hell ... what are you *doing*?"

Mum started walking towards him then. Her arm was raised, aiming the little pistol right at his head. And now Taylor started backing away. "Come on, Maria," he muttered, "don't be stupid. We can work this out ..."

But Mum just kept on walking towards him.

Taylor started circling off to one side. Mum followed him. Taylor looked behind, moved to his left. Mum moved with him. He was heading away from us all now, backing away towards the right-hand side of the roof. He was trying to keep away from the edge, but Mum kept cutting him off. She was pushing him closer and closer to the edge, and in the end he had nowhere else to go. He stopped. Mum stopped in front of him. He turned his head and gazed down over the edge.

"You're on your own now, Jack," Mum said to him.

He smiled at her. "I always was." He glanced over at Danny and Streak and the others. They were all just staring at him. He shook his head and looked back at Mum. "Do you really think I need any of them?" he said to her. "They're nothing – all of them. Less than nothing. Just like the rest of the animals round here." He grinned at Mum. "I don't need shit like that. I don't need *nothing*."

A dim pop suddenly cracked through the air. I watched as a small red hole appeared in the middle of Taylor's forehead. For one second, he just stood there in the falling snow – his shocked eyes staring, his mouth hanging open – and then he slowly toppled backwards and vanished over the edge of the roof.

CHAPTER 9
THE TRUTH

Everyone who was there that night knew it was Danny who'd shot Jack Taylor. But so far Danny hasn't been charged with anything, and I'm pretty sure that he never will be. The police are still looking into Taylor's death, but no one's talking to them. No one was there when it happened. No one saw anything. No one knows anything.

The police don't have any evidence.

And, as Taylor told me, without evidence, there's no proof. And if you don't have any proof, you might as well give up.

Now that Taylor's dead, though, people are beginning to talk about him, and the police have re-opened the investigation into Dad's death. They're also looking into what happened to Robbie Franks, and I've heard rumours that Sonia Cherry is under investigation too.

Everything's a bit weird at the moment. Our flat's still in a mess after Dev and his boys trashed it. The rioting has stopped but the estate hasn't settled down yet. Everyone's edgy. It looks like the E Boys are taking control, but there are still a few fights to be fought. And the police keep coming round to talk to us about Taylor and Dad ... and Mrs Hood has banned me from seeing Della *again*.

But I know that when everything settles down a bit, I will get round to asking Mum if Pippa Cherry is my sister. I know it's going to be really difficult, and I'm not looking forward to it.

But you have to find out the truth, don't you?

That's what it's all about.

The truth.

Our books are tested
for children and young people by
children and young people.

Thanks to everyone who consulted on
a manuscript for their time and effort in
helping us to make our books better
for our readers.